Just The Two Of Us

Forever Yours Faithfully Book One

Lisa L. Osborne

Capricorn Creations

Copyright © 2023 by Lisa L. Osborne

All rights reserved.

No portion of this book may be reproduced in any form without written permission from the publisher or author, except as permitted by U.S. copyright law.

This story is dedicated to my beloved mother, Sherry Osborne, whose illness was the inspiration, and to my beloved father, John Osborne. I'll always treasure the nineteen years we had together. I miss you both and hope you would be proud of me.

Love always,

Punky

Chapter One

CJ's hand shook as she unlocked the door to her tiny New York City apartment. It wasn't in the best of neighborhoods, but that wasn't the fear making her hand tremble. She had just received the most life-changing news of her short twenty-three years. She was pregnant. Celeste Justine Cast—or CJ—dropped her keys on a cheap table by the door and stumbled into her apartment.

"I need a hit!"

Her mother, Helen, was due to come over, and she wasn't ready to deal with her. CJ loved her mother and her stepfather, Jesse, but she needed to talk to David—her boyfriend and the baby's father. She walked over to the avocado green phone hanging on the wall and dialed the seven digits she'd been dialing for the last four years.

The door to the apartment opened, and Helen groaned as she pushed the door wide, shoving a mix of trash, clothes, and newspapers on the floor closer to the wall. "CJ! You need to clean up here! You're going to get rats!"

"Oh, Mom," CJ groaned and hung up the phone. "I'm a grown woman! I don't need you to tell me what to do."

"No, but you sure need me when you want money! I told you, CJ, you have got to stop doing drugs."

"I can stop whenever I want." CJ lit up a cigarette to calm her nerves.

"What did the doctor say?"

"I'm pregnant."

"Oh, Celeste Justine," Helen whispered.

"Don't worry, Mom, you won't have to take care of it. I'll take care of it."

"How are you going to take care of a baby? You can't even take care of yourself!"

"I don't need this now, Mom!" She stormed off to her room to be alone.

"CJ Cast, now we're going to have to talk about this." Helen followed her to the bedroom. "You need to straighten your act up! You need to get off drugs. You need to get out of here and get a good job. We can help. Do it for the baby, CJ. Do you want to bring a baby up in this environment?"

CJ looked around at the lava lamps and paraphernalia in the room and flopped onto her bed which had a spring poking out.

"Honey, let us help you."

"What can you do? I'm a total screw-up."

"Honey, we need to get you clean. We need to get you away from David. Have you told him?"

"I haven't seen him in a couple days."

"Oh, I hate that man. Look what he's done to my precious little girl." Helen sat down next to her daughter, who had softened and was tearing up.

"Should I give the baby up for adoption?"

"No, honey. We'll work together and make sure it has a good life. We'll get you cleaned up and get you in a better place. When are you due?"

"January."

"A New Year's baby." Helen smiled.

"It's a boy. I'm having David's son."

"Oh, honey." Helen wrapped her arms around her daughter, and CJ laid her head on her mom's shoulder.

"Do you think he'd marry me?"

"You don't want to marry David, CJ. He's not worth it."

"But I love him."

"You love what he gives you, honey. You don't love him. You love the drugs he plies you with. We need you to get clean, so this baby has a fighting chance. Jesse and I can help. We can get you into rehab and out of your dead-end job, and you can go to night school and make a life for yourself. Then you can find a better apartment and a better crowd to be around. Don't you want that for your son?"

"Yeah, I don't want him to grow up like this. He deserves so much more. I'm so scared, Mom." She started to cry and hid her face in her hands.

"It's okay, baby. We'll get you in a better place. You'll be able to handle things better. I'll talk to Matthew and see if he can help us. He respects Jesse and loves him. He'll help us get through everything. Are you ready to quit the drugs?" Matthew was Matthew Patrick, Jesse's stepson from his first marriage but no relation to CJ.

"Yeah, I have to do something. I don't want the baby to live like this. It's not fair to him. Do you think I can be a good mom?"

"I think you can be a great mom. You have to straighten out your act."

"I want to do that, but I need help."

"We'll help you, baby."

"I love you, Mom."

"I love you, too."

CJ went to meet David at his apartment. He sat there with his white fringed shirt unbuttoned down to his navel. He had long, curly, blond hair and a blue bandana wrapped around his forehead. His jeans had bell bottoms that flared at the ankles as he sat cross-legged on his couch, smoking cigarettes and burning incense. Lava lamps in red, blue, and green were scattered throughout the house, their ooze floating up and sinking in a hypnotic rhythm.

"Hey, baby. I haven't seen you around in a few days." David looked at CJ with his piercing, light grey eyes. "How have you been doing?" He stood up, took her hand, and pulled her back to the couch.

"David, we need to talk."

"I have just what you need right here." He handed her a bag. CJ was tempted. She had been sober for a week, though, so she handed him the bag back and slowly pushed it away. "Hey, more for me if you don't want any." He took a long puff on his cigarette.

"David, I'm pregnant."

"Pregnant? Wow, what a bummer." He took a drink of his beer. "Who's the dad?"

"You."

"I'm not the dad. You were on the pill remember?" He took another puff of his cigarette.

"Yeah, well, I'm pregnant. So what are we going to do about it?"

"Get it taken care of. There are clinics you can go to now. I know a guy."

"I'm not going to have an abortion!"

"Give it up for adoption."

"I'm not giving the baby up for adoption!"

"Babe, I don't know what you want me to do."

"I want you to be a man for a change and help me take care of this baby!"

"Sorry, man. That sounds like not a groovy thing to do. You have that mom of yours and those rich people she hangs out with. Have them take care of the baby?" He put his cigarette out and lit up a joint instead.

"So, you're not going to help me raise this baby?"

"I don't care about no baby. You got into this mess; get yourself out of it."

Before she could even consider her actions, CJ slapped him, plucked the joint from his mouth, and put it out on his pant leg.

"You bitch!"

David grabbed her and threw her to the ground. He backhanded her across the face, and she doubled over to protect the baby. He grabbed her by the hair and yanked her towards the door. She punched him as hard as she could, but he blackened her eyes. Fearing that he would hurt the baby, she stood up as he grabbed her arm and threw open the door.

"Get out of here, you slut! I don't want to ever see you again!" She blinked as the door slammed right in her face. Tears flowing down her cheeks, she placed her hand gently on her belly and promised to protect her baby at all costs. She vowed then she'd try as hard as she could to take back the control she had given up to David.

Chapter Two

Several months later, as CJ lay dreaming of floating in a lake, with the ripples tickling her feet, a sharp, stabbing pain shocked her awake. She groaned, screamed, and realized the water wasn't only in her dream. Her water had broken, and she was lying in a puddle. CJ panicked and called 911. The paramedics arrived quickly and rushed her to the hospital. Lucas James Ashton came out screaming on a frosty January morning.

Helen smiled at her grandson as he looked up at her curiously. "He's so precious, CJ." She held him in her arms. "He's perfect! He looks like you. Gorgeous with a full head of blond hair."

"I love him, Mom." CJ was glowing. "Lucas is the reason I'm going to stay clean. We're going to make a life for ourselves."

"I believe you can, baby. You can do anything you put your mind to, Celeste. I'll be here for you. Me and Jesse will be here for you."

After several months, things had been going better for CJ, but she started to use again.

"CJ, you have to do something! You can't provide for Lucas keeping this up! Now, come on, straighten yourself out! Do you have any diapers for him?"

"Yeah, they're in my bedroom," she said. She was strung out and lying on the couch.

Helen rummaged around, looking for diapers. She couldn't find any and quickly grew frustrated, but what she found instead enraged her—all kinds of drug paraphernalia.

"That does it! I'm going to take this baby and raise him myself! You don't care about him. If you did, you'd get yourself clean!"

"I'm trying, Ma. I'm trying."

"You're not trying! You're sitting there thinking about your next hit. You've seen David again, haven't you? Has he even been to see him?"

"He's busy."

"He's busy getting high is what he's busy doing! He should help you take care of his son instead of getting high and shooting you up with drugs."

"Can we stop the sermon?"

"No! Now, you said you wanted to get clean."

"Fine! I'll get clean!" she snapped. "Let me have my son!" She pulled Lucas from Helen's arms.

"I've had it, Celeste! Jesse and I are going to Kentucky, and I'm taking Lucas with me. I can't leave him here with you. I can't risk it."

"I'll be fine!"

"Honey, please let us help you." Helen pleaded.

"You don't want to help me. I'm not worthy of help." She turned away from her mother with Lucas in her arms.

"Baby, you are so worthy of help. I will not give up on you. I love you. Would you give up on Lucas if something like this happened to him?"

"No, I love him. He's my little man." She held onto her son. "I don't know what I'd do without my son."

Lucas looked up at his mom and smiled brightly. He bounced around in her arms and played with the rattle he loved so much.

"Baby, let me get with Matthew and see if we can get you some help. He might be able to get you a job, and you can leave this place. We can all move—be a fresh start for all of us. I'm sure he wouldn't mind. Will you do that?"

"What about David?"

"Baby, he uses you."

"How would you know? You have a perfect marriage."

"CJ," she sighed, tired of having this argument with her.

CJ looked at Lucas as he shook his rattle. She didn't want to fight with her mother any longer. "I need to give him a bath."

CJ headed towards the bathroom, tripping, and almost dropping Lucas.

Helen picked up the needle CJ had tripped over and shoved it in CJ's face. "What if Lucas picked that up?? Huh?! Are you willing to risk it?" Helen threw the needle in the trash forcefully and slammed the door as she walked out of the bathroom.

CJ, feeling defeated, wiped her eyes as Lucas looked up at her. He smiled his beautiful smile as CJ ran the water in the tub and set him in it. As Lucas played around in the bubbles, his mom washed him tenderly and sang to him. "I sure do love you, Luca. You're my little man. I will always love you." She sang the Dolly Parton song to her son. Lucas looked up at his mom and splashed around. "Luca, I don't know who's getting a bigger bath, you or me." She laughed as he splashed her again. "Maybe Gigi is right. Maybe we should see about moving to Kentucky and getting away from here. You deserve so much better than me as a mom. I love you, baby. I love you with all my heart."

After putting Lucas to bed, CJ went back into the living room. The urge to shoot up flowed through her veins. The need, craving, and desire ran through her. She saw her old teddy bear that Lucas now played with. "What happened to me?" She held it close to her and cried. "I have to do this. I have to get clean," she whispered, wiping the tears on her sleeve. She put the bear in Lucas's crib and then returned to the living room.

Moments later, David barged in the front door with some friends in tow. "Hey, babe," he kissed her, "let's party!" He handed her a beer while everyone lounged all over the floor, lighting up and getting high. CJ's resolve immediately evaporated. It just wasn't the right time to quit yet.

When Helen came over the next morning, she could hear Lucas crying before she even opened the door. She found the bodies of David, CJ, and their friends, passed out and littering the entire living room. CJ's 'friends' didn't belong in the same home as her grandson. "CELESTE JUSTINE!" Helen screamed. "What the hell is going on here?! Get these people out of here!" She shook a black haired hippy and woke him up. "Get out of here!" Slowly but surely, she got everyone out of the apartment. "I've had it! I'm taking Lucas, and we're going to Kentucky," Helen said, exasperated. "Can't you hear him crying? He needs changed! And I bet you spent the last bit of your money on drugs instead of diapers."

"There are cloth diapers in the bathroom."

"Oh, Celeste!" Helen marched off to tend to Lucas. "I thought you wanted to get clean?" she said, disappointed, as she walked back into the living room.

"I know. I screwed up." CJ dropped her head down in tears. "Maybe you should take Lucas so he's not a screw-up like me."

"We can get you help. You have to want to clean up."

"Do you think Matthew will let me move down there and get a decent job? I'll clean Evergreen." Evergreen Estate was where the Patricks lived.

"Yeah, Jesse's going to talk to him when we go down there. But until we get back, you have got to stay away from David."

"I will, Mom. Thank you."

"I love you, CJ."

"I love you too, Mom."

Helen picked up Lucas's things and walked out the door.

Chapter Three

Evergreen Estate was a grand palatial home that had been in the Patrick name for generations. The main family who resided there was the matriarch and owner, Mrs. Deidre Patrick, her grandson Matthew Patrick, and his wife, Dr. Melinda Heat Patrick, who was pregnant with their daughter.

Matthew and his brother John loved Jesse. He helped raise the boys after their father died, and they considered him their father. Matthew, the older of the two, was CEO of Patrick Industries. He was a multimillionaire with connections all over the globe. Everyone held him in high esteem and referred to him as Mr. Patrick. He was a tall, brooding man with dark hair and broad shoulders. He had shadowy, menacing eyes, and his voice dripped with authority—never taking no for an answer. While he was an ambitious businessman, he was also so generous that people overlooked his temper, and those closest to him always knew one wrong word could make their life hell.

"Right this way, ma'am." The chauffeur opened the door and let Jesse and Helen out of the limo. He brought around Lucas's stroller and helped Helen strap him in.

"This place gets bigger and bigger every time I come here," Helen admitted as she stepped out of the elevator at the top story. After getting settled in their room, Helen slipped off her shoes and changed into dinner attire. "I don't know why we have to dress up; we're the guests."

"I know, but Matthew has a Representative from Connecticut for dinner tonight and wants us to dress accordingly."

"Is he ever not having dinner with a Representative?"

"I understand, but remember why we're here. We're here to ask for help with CJ," Jesse reminded her.

"I know." She sighed again.

"Besides, he loves and respects you."

"I know, and it will be nice to see Melinda."

"Now, she's one I'm not too fond of. He could do so much better than that gold-digging harlot," Jesse grumbled.

"Jesse," Helen admonished.

"Well, she is. He surely can see that she's only with him so she can get her hands on this place."

"Well, he's not stupid. I'm sure he has an iron-clad prenup. Remember, he tried to get us to sign one."

"I know," he chuckled. "I said the only prenup I need is what's in my heart, and that's you, my love." He kissed Helen.

After changing, everyone went to the grand dining room for dinner. While Matthew and Representative Jackson talked business, Helen, Melinda, and Deidre retired to the drawing room.

"Gigi!" Lucas waved and smiled. He held up his rattle to show her, shaking it with pure joy. The maid came into the room with tea. Lucas shook his rattle and giggled at her. He continued shaking it until she looked at him. Then he smiled and waited until someone else came in.

"He's going to be something when he gets older," Deidre said.

"He already doesn't take no for an answer." Helen laughed as Lucas half-crawled over to Melinda, kissed her belly, and wrapped his arms around her.

"Aww," Melinda cooed. "You like the baby?"

He nodded and kissed her belly again.

"Oh, she likes you, too. I can feel her moving in my stomach." She took Lucas's hand and put it on her belly. The baby moved. Lucas laughed and bounced up and down with excitement. "Her name is Liliana. She likes you, too."

"Yes, I think it would be great for everyone—"

Matthew entered the drawing room, speaking over his shoulder to Jesse. "... You know I'd do anything for you."

"Thanks, son. I appreciate it."

"What's going on?" Deidre asked.

"We're going to get Celeste into a rehab center and move everyone down here. The baby will have a friend to grow up with."

"Oh, thank you, Matthew! Thank you so much. I'll find a way to repay you myself," Helen said.

"Don't worry about it, Helen. I am happy to do anything I can to help. And how is this little one here?" Matthew leaned over to see Lucas on his level. "You're going to grow up to be quite the businessman, I tell you. I hear no one can say no to you already."

Lucas flailed his arms at Matthew and waddled back over to Melinda, wrapping his arms around her belly and kissing it again. "Liliana already has a best friend, and she's not even born," Matthew laughed as Lucas wrapped his arms around Melinda.

"I can see them growing up together. Liliana and Lucas. I think they are going to take the world by storm." Matthew grinned at the little boy.

"That they are, Matthew. That they are," Jesse said.

Chapter Four

After their weekend in Kentucky, the holidays came. Lucas was excited for Christmas but at his first birthday party he was thrilled to be the center of attention. He loved to make people laugh and have them coo over him. CJ handed him his cake then CJ, Helen, and Jesse sang "Happy Birthday."

"Blow out the candles!" Lucas was so proud when everyone clapped for him.

CJ took the candle off. "Eat it." Everyone gathered around with Polaroid and took snapshots of Lucas sticking his fingers in the cake. Then he picked the cake up and smashed it all over his face before dropping it back on his tray. Everyone laughed and cheered; he was happy to make people smile.

Lucas's party was a success. As she put him in his crib, CJ sang to him "I Will Always Love You." That was their song. Lucas liked hearing her sing. CJ still occasionally liked to play her saxophone. Lucas loved it, especially when she played *Sweet Caroline* and did the "dun-dun-dun" noises. He would bounce around on the beat, which made her laugh.

A few days later, CJ had a rough day at work. Days like this made it hard to stay clean. Since she went into rehab, she hadn't had so much as a beer. She was proud of herself. Clean for seventy-two days. But she needed something to calm her jagged nerves and wanted a hit in the worst way.

Instead, she called her sponsor.

"Seventy-two days, CJ! That's amazing. That's something to be proud of! You can do it. You're on your way, and before you know it, you'll be reaching your ninety days, then your six months, then your year. You can do this. I know you can do this! Look how far you've come, and you don't want to go back now. Soon you'll be moving to Kentucky and starting your life over. Look what you have to look forward to. Look at your little boy. Think how much he means to you. Do you want him to grow up without you?"

"No."

"Exactly! You can do this, girl. Just fight the urges. I know it's hard, but that's what I'm here for. Lean on me when it gets too hard. I got you."

Seventy-two days.

A few days later, a man groped CJ when she was waiting tables. Caught off guard, CJ decked him and then stood there, aghast, for a few moments while the man's wife yelled for the manager. The manager had seen the whole thing, but, instead of standing up for her, he apologized to the patron.

"Eric! He groped me!"

"I don't care! He is a customer!"

"I should file charges against you for assault!" the wife of the customer yelled, then Eric turned to CJ and told her to get out.

"What?"

"You heard me; get out of here!"

"Let me get my things and my tips."

"No! You don't get your tips. Take your coat and your purse, get out of here, and don't come back!"

Once again, CJ was out of a job, and rent was due the next day. She was counting on that night's tips, too. On top of that, Lucas needed some milk, and she was sick of asking her mom for help. She already owed her from the last time she was fired. CJ was trapped in a hole with no way to get out.

The blustery, icy wind pricked at her skin as she walked the five blocks to her apartment. Her legs were freezing below her thin waitress uniform, and she wanted to take a shower after having that guy put his dirty hands on her. *God, what I wouldn't do for a hit? Seventy-seven days. Keep remembering that; seventy-seven days.* Desperate, CJ called her sponsor several times to no avail.

Figures, she thought. CJ sat on her bed and cried. The heat was out again, and she began to shiver. Jesse had the magic touch, though, and she knew he could always get it working. She would ask him when she picked up Lucas, but right now she just wanted a bath, a long, hot bath.

Seventy-seven days. Remember that CJ; seventy-seven days.

Jesse and Helen brought Lucas home, saving CJ the trip. After only a few minutes, Jesse was able to get the heater working, enough time for Helen to worm out what happened at the restaurant. She made it pretty clear she didn't believe CJ's version of the events.

"Oh, thanks for the vote of confidence, Mom!"

"CJ!"

"No, don't CJ me! He groped me! I had every right to deck him."

"But you lost your job."

"I'll figure something out."

"I can loan you the rent money, but you have to pay me back."

"I'll pay you back when we get to Kentucky and I get to work for Matthew. Do you know what he's going to have me do?"

"I don't know," Jesse sighed. "But you know, honey, your mom and I are going out on a limb for you here."

"Not you, too," CJ said, exasperated. "I'll pay you guys back."

"It's not that, love. We want you to get better."

"I'm seventy-seven days sober! In thirteen days I'll have reached three months! Can't you be excited and happy for me about that? Can one of you at least pretend to be proud of me? I know I've made some mistakes, but I'm trying to do better."

"I am proud of you, butterfly. I am so proud of you."

"Thanks, Daddy." She hugged him and held onto him. "I love you."

"I love you too, Butters."

"Butters." CJ chuckled.

"Are you packing up what you don't need?" Helen looked around.

"Yeah. I have an area just for stuff I'm going to get rid of when we move. I'm excited about the move. I think this is the fresh start we all need."

"I'm sorry I got so upset with you. I know you're trying as hard as you can."

"Some days it feels like I can do no right."

"I get that, my little star. You'll have days like that."

"Thanks for getting the heat to work again." She hugged Jesse.

"You're welcome, Butters."

"Well," Helen sighed and stood up, "it looks like we fixed everything. I'll come by in the morning to check on you, and we'll continue to pack stuff."

"Okay. I love you, Mom."

"I love you, too, CJ."

CJ sat on the couch, staring at the TV. At the age of twenty-four, she could feel the heavy burden of the world on her shoulders. She dropped her head in her hands. *I feel horrible having to bum money from my mom. I'll never get her paid back. I can't wait to move to Kentucky and start fresh. Tomorrow is day seventy-eight. Two weeks till we move to Kentucky. I can't take this pressure! He's only got two diapers left. What am I going to do? I want a cold Bud. A Bud and a cigarette. That would ease my mind. Thirteen days till I reach ninety days! I can do this. I have to be strong. For Lucas, I have to be strong. I can do it for you, baby. Stay strong, CJ, stay strong.*

CJ put Lucas to bed and then heard a knock at her door.

"Hey, CJ, it's me," David Ashton whispered from behind the door. It had been nearly three months since she'd last seen him.

She opened the door and stood in the opening, scowling at him. "Go away," she grumbled.

"Look, baby, I need you to get me some stuff. I'm in for it bad. You know Charlie. Have him get you the good stuff."

"Look, David, I'm clean! I haven't done anything in seventy-seven days."

"Now, CJ, you know you're not clean, baby. You tell everyone that. You just let everyone think that. Come on, now, I need it bad, man."

"Get it yourself."

"I told you, woman! Get it for me!" He slapped her across the face, knocking her off her feet.

CJ wasn't one to cower. She got back up and punched him in the gut. "I said get! Get out of my house! Get out of my house before I call the cops."

"And tell them what? You're just a junkie like me. What are they going to do? I tell you what they're going to do; they're going to take your kid away for being a damn junkie! Now get me my stuff, and I'll leave."

"Get it yourself!"

"Call him or else."

"Or else what?"

"Celeste!"

"David!"

He reached out and slapped her again. David was stubborn, and she knew she wouldn't be able to get him to leave unless she did what he said. She wanted to call the cops, but the threat of having Lucas taken away terrified her. So she gave in.

Charlie made a late-night call to her house. It had been seventy-seven days since she'd seen him. Seventy-seven days since she'd put money in his pocket. He slipped her a little baggy of white powder, a tourniquet, and a needle. He had a six-pack in one hand and was smoking a fat rolled joint, with the other. The feeling of the needle and tourniquet in her hand sent all the old memories flooding back. The need, the ache, and the desire returned in full force. *Stay strong, Celeste!*

The devil in Charlie encouraged her to go for it. The devil in David reminded her she was just a junkie. With one of them standing on either side of her, was reminded her of her past. She eyed David. His orange shirt was unbuttoned and had a collar protruding from his jacket, and the pants he wore were yellow polyester bell-bottom pants. She turned to Charlie, with his afro and beads hanging down his chest like Jimi Hendrix.

"Just one hit, baby. That's all you need, just one hit. It's not gonna hurt you. This is the mild stuff. Just one hit, baby." David's voice kept ringing in her ears.

CJ had to battle against the urge. She needed someone to bring her back from this dark place, this dark pit of despair. She needed to fight for Lucas, but the longer she held onto the items, the stronger the urge became. If she ever needed someone in her corner, it was now, but these two were the only ones she had.

Charlie handed her the beer she'd been so desperate for. She held the cold, amber bottle in her hands, letting the condensation drip down her fingers. She lifted it to her lips. *Seventy-seven days!* Her instincts were telling her to stop, but the cool liquid traipsed across her pink, chapped lips, and she began to feel free again. She took a long drink.

"That's it, girl! That's it! Drink it down," Charlie encouraged her.

She drank the rest of the bottle in one swig. "Ahhhh." She smiled. When she handed him the bottle back, he had another one ready for her.

CJ was ready, too. She wanted more. She needed the release.

"Just one hit, baby. Just one hit," David kept encouraging her. He called some friends to come over, and after seventy-seven days, so close to the peak, CJ fell from her mountain.

Chapter Five

Lucas's crying echoed through the apartment building. CJ's neighbor, Stacey, banged on the door to see if she could do anything to get him to quiet down. "CJ?" The door creaked open, an eerie sound. Cold air blasted through the room, sending a shiver down her spine. Stacey made her way towards the bedroom where Lucas was wailing. "CJ?" She called out again, and, opening the bedroom door, she gasped at what she saw.

"CJ!" Stacey ran over to where her friend was lying on the floor and rolled her over. A tourniquet was on her arm, and her half-opened glazed-over eyes stared up at the ceiling. Stacey felt for a pulse, but there was none. "Oh, CJ," she said, sadly.

Stacey picked Lucas up. "It's okay, little man. I got you. We'll get you changed." After she held him close and gave him a toy, he calmed down long enough for Stacey to call 911.

When the cops came to the apartment, Officer Wanda West tended to CJ while Officer Ron Ward took Stacey's statement.

"So sad she was so young. Is this her son?"

"Yeah, this is Lucas."

"Hi, little man." Officer Ward looked at the little boy. His cheeks were tear-stained and red. He stared back at the officer, confused. "Ma'am, it's best if we take you out of here. We have someone from CPS on the way to take care of the little one."

"His grandmother should come over soon."

"Do you know what her name is?"

"Helen Thompson."

"Do you know how to get ahold of her?"

"I don't. I'm sorry."

"How about you go with Officer West here back to your apartment, and we'll come back when CPS gets here." Officer West came over and escorted her out of the room.

Officer Ward looked around, fuming over the circumstances. It was the third overdose that week, and they'd gotten there too late to save the mother. "Stupid fucking drugs!" He grew infuriated as he waited in the hall for Dr. Pickett to come retrieve the body. "She was so beautiful! So young and had such a life ahead of her. To leave behind a baby, too. Oh, I hate my job sometimes." He sighed.

Dr. Pickett made her presence known with a little cough. "Hey, Ron."

"Hey, Janice. Right this way." He led her down the hall to the bedroom on the right.

"So sad," she whispered as she bent over to look at the woman. While she did her investigation, CPS arrived.

Officer Ward had just returned from the neighbor's apartment when someone else came to the door. "What are …?" She looked around. "What's going on?"

"Who are you, ma'am?"

Helen searched the living room in a panic. "I'm Helen Thompson. This is my daughter's apartment. What's going on? Where's ... where's my CJ? CJ!"

"Ma'am, have a seat, please."

Helen stared at him with big, scared eyes. "What is going on?" she asked again.

Jesse entered the apartment, looking confused. "What's ..."

Helen gaped at her husband, terrified. "Jesse," she gasped and reached her hand out to him. He sat next to her and squeezed her hand.

"Ma'am ... sir," Officer Ward started softly. "I'm so sorry."

"Sorry?" Helen asked. "Sorry about what? What happened?"

Before Officer Ward could tell them anything, Dr. Pickett and her assistant rolled the body past them and out the door.

"NO!" Helen screamed.

"I'm so sorry for your loss," Officer Ward said.

"NO!!" Helen shook her head. "No!! No!! No!!!" she kept screaming. "Not my CJ! NO!"

"I'm so sorry, ma'am." Helen fell off the couch and onto her knees, begging the universe for it to be a mistake. "Not my CJ!!! No! Please no! Not my CJ! My CJ!" She dropped her head in her hands and sobbed.

Jesse got on the floor with her, wrapped his arms around her, and held her as she called out in pain. "She's dead, Jesse! She's dead!" She screamed into his shoulder. "My CJ is dead! She was doing so well, too. She had gotten help and was off drugs, and now she's dead!" Jesse held her tight, trying to be strong for his wife.

"Is there anyone you want us to call for you?" Officer Ward offered kindly.

"No, thank you. Can I see her?"

"I'll take you down there when you're ready."

"Where's Lucas?" Helen looked around.

"He's with an officer down the hall."

"He's all I have left of my daughter."

"I'm so sorry for your loss. We'll be in touch with some follow-up questions," Officer Ward told them.

Everything was coming at Helen at once, and it was overwhelming. "I need to see Lucas."

"Yes, of course. Let me escort you to him."

Helen took one look at Lucas and rushed to take him from a grateful Stacey. "Oh, my baby boy!" she cried as she held him close.

"Gigi!" She kissed his head and squeezed him tight. "I love you, Lucas." She cradled him in her arms.

"Gigi!" Lucas cooed at her, finally calm for the first time that morning.

"Yes, Gigi is here. Oh, my darling Lucas. I love you with everything in my soul. We're going to get through this together. You and me; we're a team."

When the officers and CPS were finished with their questions, Jesse and Helen took Lucas to their house to start their lives over.

Chapter Six

Matthew, Helen, and Jesse were the new owners of Thompson's Cleaners and Laundromat. Lucas, now four years old, loved going into the laundromat and talking to the ladies, like the big man he was. He was a great helper, handing them towels and anything he could reach. One day, there was a little boy Lucas's age there with his mother. Helen smiled as Lucas went up to him and started talking to him. They hit it off and played with their cars.

"Oh, shit!" Helen spilled some laundry detergent. Before she could clean it up, Lucas and the little boy went over to the spilled laundry detergent, took their Matchbox cars, and drove them through it.

"Snow!" Lucas laughed.

"Now, Jacob Isaac!" The boy's young mother yelled as she saw what was going on. "Now I have to clean you off!" The mother took Jacob to the sink and rinsed off his knees. "Sometimes, son, I don't know what I'm going to do with you." She put him down and went back to sorting through her laundry again, while Jacob went back to Lucas.

The boys wiped off their cars and continued to play. "I'm glad he's got a friend to play with now," the other mother told Helen.

"I'm glad Lucas does, too."

"This is Jacob. I'm Elizabeth Glass." She reached out her hand to shake Helen's.

"Helen."

"Nice to meet you, Helen."

"You, too."

Helen and Elizabeth talked while they waited for their clothes to finish. Helen looked Elizabeth over. She was around CJ's age but a little shorter, with blond hair and baby-blue eyes. Jacob looked just like her and wore glasses. He and Lucas had become instant friends. Helen loved watching them play together. For the first time in a long time, she remembered CJ without the pain. She imagined CJ in the laundromat, with Lucas helping her fold clothes. She was always happy to see Elizabeth and Jacob Glass when they came in every Wednesday.

It was another slow day when Lucas heard the bell on the door jingling. "Jake!" Lucas ran to him, and they hugged. They sat down at Helen's feet to play with their cars, but, before long, the boys found some mischief to get into. Lucas and Jacob were drawn to some spilled detergent like moths to a flame, running their cars through it and spreading the mess on themselves and across the floor.

"Now, little boy," Elizabeth scolded Jacob, "how many times do I have to tell you to not get in the detergent?"

Jacob snickered as Elizabeth pulled him over to the sink and washed his hands and knees, only for Jacob to run back over to Lucas and do it again. Helen got exasperated at them, but all they could do was laugh.

"Boys will be boys," Elizabeth chuckled. "How are you doing, Lucas?"

"I'm fine. How are you?"

"You're such a smooth talker, aren't you?"

Lucas flashed his charming smile and giggled. He talked to Elizabeth like he had known her all his life; she talked to him like he was her son. Jacob asked Lucas where his mom was.

"She passed away," Helen said.

"I am so sorry," Elizabeth whispered. "We didn't know."

"It's okay."

"How are you doing?"

"Each day is hard, but I try to hold on for Lucas. He was a year old when she passed. You remind me of her. She would be around your age. I see you, and it reminds me of her so much. I look forward to you coming in on Wednesdays to do your laundry. If there's anything I can do, let me know. I want to take care of you since I can't take care of my CJ."

"I couldn't ask you for anything."

"I mean it."

"I appreciate it."

Elizabeth counted her quarters and put some of the clothes back. "Maybe next week." Helen noticed she always washed her waitress uniforms and a few of Jacob's clothes, but she often put back her linens and towels. She overheard Jacob asking her about the soup kitchen and noticed growls coming from their stomachs. She watched Elizabeth split her sandwich with Jacob and give the rest to Lucas when he told her he was hungry. Helen knew that was all she had. *She gave all she had to those kids. Who knows when she'll get to eat? Okay, it's time I step in.*

"Hand me your dirty clothes," Helen ordered Elizabeth. Elizabeth gaped at her, confused. "Hand them to me."

Elizabeth did as she was told. Helen put them in the washer and started a load. "Helen," Elizabeth said, shocked. "I don't have the money to pay for that."

"Don't worry about it. You're my family, I can't let you not get your clothes washed. Now, come on, I'm getting something to eat. Do you like Chinese food?"

"Yes, I love it, but I can't afford it."

"Don't worry about it. It's payday. You can buy when you can."

"Thank you," Elizabeth said softly. "I was afraid I wouldn't be out of here before the soup kitchen closed. I didn't get off work till late, and I had to do laundry."

"You're coming home with me tonight. We're going to get you some decent food."

"Helen, I can't ask you to do that."

"Nonsense! My CJ was a waitress, and she would want me to take care of you like I would her. Maybe you can watch Lucas for me sometime."

"Absolutely! I'll watch him anytime you need me to."

"I appreciate it. Sometimes it gets to be too much."

"I understand. Sometimes it's hard with Jacob. He has to come into the diner with me when I work my shifts, and it's hard worrying about a three-year-old."

"Is his dad around?"

"His dad bailed on me as soon as he found out I was pregnant."

"Oh, some men," Helen grumbled.

"It's okay. The Lord has always provided for me. He's never let me down, and He won't start now. My mom died when Jake was a year old. It's always been just the two of us."

"Well, not now. Now you have a family that loves and cares for you. I'll take Jacob when you go to work. Just drop him off, and, when you get off work—if you don't mind—you can take Lucas for a little while."

"That'd be great! Thank you so much."

"We're going to get you taken care of, sweet girl."

"I told you He will always provide. He's never let me down. I have faith everything will be okay." Elizabeth smiled brightly at Helen.

While Helen wasn't religious, Elizabeth was a newly converted born-again Christian. She said she could lose everything in the world but never lose her faith, no matter how badly she was tested. Elizabeth witnessed to Helen several times and spent her free time reading the beloved Bible her mom left her. She read to the boys until Lucas asked her too many questions. "Lulu, I have to read my Bible to find out." Lucas cackled.

With business picking up, Helen hired Elizabeth to be the manager and do alterations. Elizabeth liked to sew and cook, as well. There were days Helen didn't have it in her to make dinner when she got home, so she had Elizabeth over to make dinner for both of their families. Helen always sent food home so Elizabeth and Jacob could have a decent meal the next day, and Elizabeth was always grateful.

Since she started working at the laundromat, Elizabeth slowly got ahead on her rent and other bills. Jacob was now fed regularly and had reached a healthy weight. Jacob and Lucas were the best of friends. By summer, Lucas was confused and distressed that he was going away to Kentucky and having to leave Jacob and his precious *Mama G* (G standing for Glass) He was still fighting it when they were on their way to the airport.

"Jake's got to stay with his mommy," Helen explained.

"But she's my mommy, too," Lucas defended.

"She's not your mommy, Lucas. Your mommy was sick and died."

"Mama G's my mommy!" He plopped down on the floor and folded his arms. "She'll always be my mommy!"

"I know, baby but you always have fun with Lilly. Remember you get to go horseback riding."

"But I want to stay with Jake."

"I know Lucas, but you'll be back here before you know it," Helen said as she and Jesse led him onto the plane with them.

She and Jesse loved Lucas and would miss him when he was gone, but they enjoyed having him away for the summer. It was their time to get their sanity back, and they always appreciated Matthew for letting him stay with him.

A couple of hours later, the limo dropped them off at the front of Evergreen, where Lilly and Matthew waited for them.

"Hi, Grandpa!" Lilly squealed. "I'm so excited to see you!" In December she would be four, but she spoke so eloquently. "Hi, Lilly Bug, how are you?"

She giggled at the pet name. Then she saw him coming up the stairs. "LUKIE!" She bounced up and down.

Lucas smiled, let go of Helen's hand, and ran up the stairs to see his dear friend. He kissed her forehead and hugged her tightly.

"I missed you, Lukie!"

"I missed you too, Lilly."

"We get to go to Uncle John's for the summer! Oh, and I got some cool new toys to show you and our new horse—her name is Fallen Snow. She's white with little black speckles on her."

Jesse stood back and watched Lilly talk to Lucas until they ran off to play.

"Hi, Dad! Hi, Helen!" Matthew came in and hugged them both.

"She's something else. She's so smart." Jesse said of Lilly.

"We're having her IQ tested. How's Lucas doing?" Matthew asked.

"He's doing well. He has a little friend now—Jake. They are a perfect match, just like two peas in a pod. They go everywhere together. They hang out in the laundromat and play with cars. Lucas likes to go up to the little old ladies and sweet talk them." They chuckled. "He's such a charmer."

"He gets it off his grandpa." Matthew laughed.

"I'm grateful you guys do this for us every year. As we get older, sometimes it's harder to take care of him. He's so rambunctious."

"If there ever comes a time when you can't take care of him, let me know, and I'll take him in. In the future, he will be a great businessman. He has that aura about him. He knows what he wants, and he gets it. There's no stopping him. Don't worry about him, Dad. We'll take care of him."

"Thanks, son. I appreciate it." He patted Matthew on the back.

Lucas thrived while staying with Uncle John, Aunt Sheryl, Lilly, and John's kids, Joe and Mary. It was like he had his own built-in family; he was no longer the little orphan boy from New York City. There were children his age, and he'd laugh and play and get into all kinds of mischief. John and Sheryl had their hands full for the summer, but the kids loved it.

Summer ended, and it was time to return home. Matthew, Melinda, and Lilly stood on the steps at the runway to see them off. Lilly held onto her nanny's hand as tears poured down her cheeks. "I'm going to miss you, Lukie," she sobbed like her heart was being ripped out of her chest.

"I'm going to miss you, too, Lilly." He held onto her tightly, his wispy, blond hair blowing in the wind.

"Can you come see me again soon?"

"We'll be back in no time," Jesse consoled her. "We have to take Lucas home, but we'll be back in a couple of months. Can you hold out a couple of months?"

Lilly nodded heavily, and her blond pigtails bounced.

"That's my big girl. Now, give Grandpa a kiss."

She held onto him and cried her heart out. "I don't want you to go," she sobbed.

"I know, baby."

"Stay here with me."

"I can't, love. My home is in New York." Lilly crossed her arms and stomped her foot.

"Now, Liliana! Be a good Lilly Bug for Grandpa. Can you do that?"

She nodded again.

"That's my girl. If you're good, I'll let Lucas call you when he gets home."

"I'll behave myself," she gushed. "I'm always good!"

"I know you are, sweetheart. Okay, wave goodbye to me." He waved to her, took Lucas's hand, and walked over to the plane. They turned around one last time to say goodbye. Lilly was still crying, but she was brave and waving goodbye to her precious Lukie.

Chapter Seven

When Helen looked at her now eleven-year-old grandson, Lucas, as he read comics with this friend Jacob, the weight of caring for him weighed on her tremendously. *What would happen to him if something happened to us? I know Elizabeth offered, but she can barely take care of Jacob. Maybe it's time to talk to Matthew while Lucas is young enough to adapt. He could start school in the fall with Lilly.*

After Lucas and Jacob went out to play, Helen turned to Jesse. "Maybe it's time we move to Kentucky."

Jesse looked up from his newspaper and glanced over his glasses at her. "Why do you say that?"

"What would happen to Lucas if one of us got sick? He's a handful already. Can you imagine raising him as a teenager? I'm worried about your heart."

"My heart is fine. I'm sure Elizabeth would raise him."

"She can't afford to raise him and Jacob. I was just thinking about how Matthew offered to raise him. Maybe it's time we take him up on it."

"What are we going to do about Elizabeth and Jacob?"

"I know," Helen sighed. "I want to get her settled and make sure she's safe. That place they live in now isn't the safest in the world."

"Maybe she could go with us?"

"She won't want to move. Remember when we asked her to come down with us, even to visit? She always said her home is here and she had no desire to go anywhere else. She's never even left New York. I worry greatly about Lucas. He's all I have of CJ. He needs a father, and Matthew would be a good father to him."

"You're right."

"I just worry about Elizabeth and Jacob and what they're going to do. That complex isn't safe. Drugs are bad there, and it's no place for a single mom with a little boy to live. I can't leave without getting her somewhere safe."

"Is she able to get help from the government?" Jesse asked his wife of twenty years.

"She's trying, but there's a waiting list a mile long."

"If we move, I want them to have at least one more summer together," Jesse informed her.

"Yeah, me, too."

"And I want to keep in contact with them. She's like my daughter, too, and I want Lucas to still have his friend," Jesse told her.

"Absolutely," Helen agreed.

"And we need to see if we can get her someplace safe."

"Yeah," Helen sighed. "She's like my CJ."

"How are you doing with that? I know her birthday is tomorrow."

"I don't want to talk about it." Helen brushed off her pants and returned to watching TV.

"Helen, he deserves to know about his mom. He's older now, and he can understand what happened."

"No! I forbid it! It's too hard to talk about her."

"Honey ..." Jesse reasoned with her. "Jesse, I said no!"

"Do you ever think maybe I'd like to talk about her?"

"She was my daughter, and I say no."

"That's not fair!"

"I don't care. I don't want to talk about it." Helen walked away, and Jesse sighed and continued reading his newspaper.

The next day Jesse spoke with Matthew about Elizabeth. Matthew offered to buy a house for her, wherever she wanted to live, or they would make a place for her at Evergreen. When Helen told Elizabeth about the move, she was heartbroken. She'd miss Helen and her family so much, and she knew Jacob would be lost without his best friend. She was humbled by Matthew's offer, but she could never leave New York. She'd grown up there. It was all she'd ever known. Besides, her daughter Sarah, who died at six months old from SIDS, was buried there and she couldn't leave her. To Helen's sadness, Elizabeth wouldn't even consider relocating.

"Honey, I will do anything I can do to help you."

"The Lord will always provide. He has all these years." Elizabeth smiled brightly, belying her sad eyes and her shaky voice. "I'll always have faith. It's just another hurdle we have to overcome."

"I love you, baby." Helen hugged her and held her tight. "We'll get you a house."

"Tell Matthew I'll pay rent. I'll pay him back. And you know if something happened to you, I'd take Lucas in."

"Honey, you can barely take care of yourself and Jacob."

"I know, but I'd find a way. God will always provide. He's like my son. I love that little boy."

"I know, and we love you, too. The both of you mean so much to us, but we think it's time we retire and move to Kentucky. We'll keep the laundromat, and you can work there as long as you want to. So, you'll always have a job."

"I'm going to miss you." Elizabeth wiped her tears on her sleeve. "You were always a mom to me."

"You'll always be my daughter. I'll call you all the time."

"Have you told Lucas?"

"Not yet. We're giving him and Jacob this summer together, and then we'll move for the start of the new school year."

"Oh, Mama."

"Baby. No matter what, I promise to stay in touch with you. I love you, Elizabeth."

"I love you, too."

Helen found a nice house in the newspaper, and she and Jesse took Elizabeth to look at it.

Elizabeth beamed as they pulled into the driveway. "I've never lived in a house before. I've always lived in apartments. I'm not sure what to do with a house." Elizabeth stared at the place in awe. "I feel like I'm getting a mansion."

The house wasn't much, but, for someone on the verge of being homeless, it was a palace. It was a two-bedroom with white siding, a fenced-in yard, and several giant trees. The living room had floor to ceiling wood paneling, and the bathroom was painted canary yellow. The kitchen cabinets were old and dated, but the water ran, the heat worked, and there was a window air conditioner for the summer. It was much more than what they had now. She and Jacob would have their separate rooms again for the first time in years. "It's beautiful! I can make curtains to hang up. I'm so excited! We'll be able to live here for a long time. Dad, thank you so much. Thank Mr. Patrick for me. I could never repay his generosity."

"Honey, you are so welcome." Jesse wrapped his arm around Elizabeth and kissed her temple.

"I'm going to miss you so much."

"I'm going to miss you, too. I'll try to come back up and see you if possible," Jesse told her.

"I appreciate it, and I want to talk to you all the time."

"My sweet girl, we'll keep in touch." Jesse hugged her tightly.

Helen made Lucas's favorite dinner to soften the blow when she told him about their summer plans. Even though he missed Elizabeth and Jacob dearly, Lucas loved spending summers with the Patricks. He loved John and Matthew as if they were his parents. Deidre was his mhamo, and Lilly was his little sister. What Lucas, Jesse, and Helen didn't know was Matthew's heavy drinking had escalated into bad times for Lilly. Melinda, her mom, left her on John's porch when she was six years old. Matthew had grown verbally and physically abusive and threatened everyone into silence. John tried to get custody, but it was always denied because of Matthew's political power.

"Guess what, Lucas?" Helen asked casually as she took a bite of her salad.

"What, Gigi?"

"We're not going to Kentucky for the summer."

"We're not? What about Lilly? What about Uncle John?"

"We're staying here for the summer; we figured we'd let you stay here, too."

"Awesome!" Lucas high-fived Jacob. "We get to hang out all summer!"

"Totally awesome!" Jacob and Lucas did their secret handshake.

Helen watched her little family. *I'm going to shake up his and Jacob's world soon.*

"Lilly's going to be upset."

"I know, but she'll be okay. You'll be seeing her soon enough."

"That's cool. I love her. She's a cool little girl," Lucas admitted about his other best friend.

"She still your sissy?" Jesse laughed.

"She'll always be my sissy." Lucas giggled.

After the final clue on *Jeopardy*, Helen called Matthew. "Thank you for all the help with the house. Elizabeth is so appreciative of it."

"You're welcome. I wanted you to have what you needed. I'm excited you guys are moving back at the end of the summer."

"Are we doing the right thing?"

"Helen, it's the right thing. He needs a father figure in his life. What would happen to him if something happened to one of you? I know that's what you worry about."

"You'd take him in, wouldn't you?"

"That's why I'm taking him in now, so you don't have to worry about it. He'll be growing up with Liliana. I know she's going to be excited when she finds out."

"You haven't told her?"

"Not yet. I figured I'd let you tell Lucas first. I don't want her telling him without you having time to tell him."

"I appreciate it. I know how she is about blurting things out." They chuckled.

Helen called Lucas into the living room. "You can have the phone now," she told him.

"Thanks! I can't wait to talk to Lilly." Lucas pulled the cord back into his room and sat on his bed, waiting for Lilly to be on the other end of the line. They chatted for a few minutes and caught up, and, as usual, their talk became more personal.

"Lately, I've been missing my mom," Lucas confessed. "Sometimes I get jealous over people that still have their mom, and I don't have anyone."

"Lukie, you'll always have me."

"I'm grateful. You'll always have me, too." For the last couple of months, they liked to get the same book and read it to each other. "Do you still have that princess book?"

"Yeah. She is a brat!"

"Let's read our book." They spent the next twenty minutes taking turns at reading *The Diary of a Princess*.

"How did your test go?" Lilly asked.

"I aced it! Thanks for tutoring me. You should be a teacher," Lucas told her.

"I can't. Daddy tells me I have to be a neurosurgeon. He's gotten me little dolls to practice on. I want to be an architect. Remember how we'd build up tall buildings with your Legos?"

"Yes, then you'd come in and crash them down and get me in trouble for being mad. Remember that big skyscraper we built? You stubbed your toe, and it toppled down?"

"Yeah. That took a lot of time."

"Uncle John was so mad." Lucas snickered. "He was all the time stepping on them. I think he said a few words he didn't mean to." Lucas figured it was time to relay the news about summer. He knew she'd be upset. "Guess what, Lils."

"What Lukie?"

"I'm not coming down there this summer."

"WHAT?! NO! You have to come down, Lukie!"

"I know, Lilly. I'm sorry. Gigi didn't say why we're not coming down. I don't know when I'll be down again."

"But, Lukie, I miss you. I miss Gigi and Grandpa, too."

"I miss you, too, princess." He chuckled.

"Why are you calling me princess? I'm not like that girl in that book."

"I didn't say you were. You have your moments, though."

"But she was a brat. I'm not a brat."

"You have your moments," Lucas egged her on.

"Oh, yeah? Like when?"

"Oh, I can't think of any right now—Ow!" Lucas rubbed his head.

"What happened?"

"I was playing with the cord, and I fell off the bed." They laughed hysterically.

"Maybe I can come up there for the summer." Lilly said.

"Oh, that would be awesome! I'll ask Gigi and Grandpa and see what they say. I hope you can come up here and we can watch movies together—me, you, and my best friend Jake."

"I thought I was your best friend?"

"You're my best friend, too. I like you both."

"But you can't have two best friends. Then, who would be the bestest best friend?" Lilly pondered aloud.

"You just hurt my head. You both are the bestest best friends in the world. I hope you come up here. I think you two would get along."

"Will you get off the phone!" Helen called to Lucas through the door.

"Ugh, Gigi wants me off the phone. I better go."

"Ask them if I can come up this summer and stay with you."

"I'll ask. Cross your fingers."

"Got them and my toes crossed." They giggled.

"Okay, princess, I'll see you later."

"Ugh, why are you calling me princess?"

"Because you're my princess," Lucas giggled.

"I hate being called princess. She was a brat."

"Yeah, and so are you sometimes." He laughed.

"I'm not a brat! You're the brat, Lucas James!"

"Lucas!" Helen screamed again.

"Ugh, she's yelling at me. I gotta go. Talk to you later."

A couple of nights later, after Helen talked with Matthew, Lucas took the phone and went into his room to talk with Lilly. "Guess what, Lukie! I am coming up there to stay with Gigi this summer!"

"You are?"

"I am! I get to stay with you for two months. I come up in the middle of June, and I go home in the middle of August."

"That's awesome! Princess." He chuckled.

"Stop calling me princess!"

"Oh, Lils. You'll always be my princess." Lucas loved getting her wound up.

Sensing her own weakness, Lilly chose to ignore him and move on. "So, what are we going to do while I'm up there?"

"I don't know. You'll get to meet Jake."

"Your other best friend?"

"Yeah, he's my other best friend,"

"But I'm still the bestest best friend, right?"

"Yeah, princess, you are."

"I'm going to smack you for calling me princess when I get up there," she growled. Lucas laughed that much harder. "What's Jake like?"

"Oh, he's great! He's like a brother to me."

"What's his mom like?"

"Mama G? She's awesome! She's a great cook."

"Miss Sarah has been teaching me how to cook," Lilly told him. Sarah Jane Smith was the head chef at Evergreen.

"Has she?"

"Yeah, I like it! I like to make spaghetti from scratch. I like to get my hands in the dough."

"Maybe you can make my ziti and ravioli."

"I'd love to do that. I haven't made it yet. Do you think Mama G will like me?"

"She'd love you. She doesn't have any girls around."

"There are no little girls there?"

"It's just me and Jake."

"What do you like to do?"

"We like playing by the tree. And we watch scary movies, but you can't say anything to Jake. That's our secret."

"I won't. I can't wait to get there. I come up after school on the twelth."

"Too bad you won't be here for the eighth. That's Jake's tenth birthday."

"Will he like me?" Lilly asked.

"I don't see why not."

"I just hope everyone likes me."

"They will."

After dinner the next evening, Jesse and Helen skipped their nightly *Jeopardy* and *Wheel of Fortune* to have a hard conversation with Lucas. "This is it, honey." Jesse held Helen's hand.

"Let's get this over with." Helen sighed.

"Little man, we have to talk," Jesse said.

"Okay." Lucas looked at them innocently. Jesse turned the TV off and reached out and squeezed Helen's hand. "You're getting older, and ... it's getting too hard for us to take care of you."

"What do you mean?" Lucas asked in a panic, his eyes dancing between their faces. His heart raced in his chest. *What is happening!?*

"Lilly is going to come stay with us for the summer."

"She told me. She was excited."

"At the end of the summer, you're going to go back with her."

"What do you mean?"

"We're all going to move to Kentucky."

"What? NO! I want to stay here! I can stay with Jake and Mama G. Can't I stay here with them?"

"No, son, you can't," Jesse told him."But why?"

"Because they can't afford to take care of you."

"Can't they come stay with us?"

"No," Jesse said.

"Why not? Matthew has all that house. I can share my room with Jake."

"It's just ... their home is here."

"So is my home, too," Lucas pleaded with them.

"I thought you liked Lilly."

"I do, and I love Matthew and Uncle John, but my home is here."

"I'm sorry, son. We're just getting too old to take care of you. We're afraid something is going to happen to us, and then you'll not have any family." Jesse was honest with him.

"I hate my life!" Lucas screamed and ran to his room. He flopped on his bed and cried his heart out. He could feel the life he'd known turning upside down. Now, he *really* wanted a mom.

Lucas called Elizabeth, still crying. She calmed him down and told him that, no matter what happened in his life, she'd always be his

Mama G. "I don't want to leave you. I like my life here. I want to grow up with Jake."

"I know, Lulu. I don't want you to leave, either."

"Can't you come with us?"

"I wish we could, sweetheart, but you'll always have a home here."

"What am I going to do without you, Mama G?"

"You're going to grow up to be big and strong. You're going to get good grades. And you're going to make me proud, just like you do now."

"Can I call you?"

"I'd be hurt if you didn't."

"I love you, Mama G."

"I love you too, baby. Now you be strong for Gigi and Grandpa. They're worried about you. They're doing this so they don't have to worry about you."

"I know," he admitted.

"I'll always be your Mama G. If you need anything, you just call me. You hear me? And remember to always say your prayers. Do you still say your prayers?"

"Yeah. I pray for you and Jake every night."

"That's a good boy. Just remember, Lulu, look for the brightest star in the sky when things get hard. I'll think of you and wish on it."

"Thanks, Mama G." Lucas wiped his eyes.

"I love you, Lulu."

"I love you, too."

Lucas spent the rest of the night in his room alone. His world was about to change. *Why do I have to move? Why can't I stay here? Why can't they stay here?* His heart broke, as the tears rolled from his eyes. In a little over two months, he would lose everything he had ever known. His mom was going to be taken away from him yet again.

"Why do I always lose everyone I love?" he cried. "Mama," he said as he wiped his eyes, "I sure do wish you were here." He screamed into his pillow and threw it across the room. Out of nowhere, he could smell the faint scent of lavender, and he felt a tender, invisible hand on his cheek. He opened his eyes, but there was no one there. A soft breeze blew through the room, enveloping him in a warm embrace. Lucas smiled to himself. "Thanks, Mama. I love you," he said softly then went to sleep.

Chapter Eight

Lucas felt torn about the move because he had a family in New York, but he also loved his family in Kentucky and loved being around Lilly.

"Why can't you guys move with us?" Lucas asked Jacob as they walked around. "Things would be so much better if you could move with us. Matthew has that big house; he can afford to keep you."

"I know. I don't want you to leave, either. You're my brother. My big brother. Why can't they move up here? We can all go to school together."

"I don't know." Lucas picked up a rock and threw it. "Adults are so weird. I mean, everything is going fine. Why do they have to break it up now? Grandpa is doing better. His heart is fine. Why are they suddenly wanting me to move down there? Gigi said I can still call and talk to you. Maybe we can come back and visit."

"That would be awesome. Maybe you can come up for Christmas … or my birthday?"

"Yeah, I'll ask. We'll always be brothers, right?" Lucas asked.

"We'll always be brothers. Avengers promise!" They made fists and did their secret handshake.

When June twelfth finally rolled around, Lilly was put on a plane, and Jesse, Helen, and Lucas met her at the airport. When the door to the plane opened, out walked a ten-year-old girl with blond pigtails. Lilly held her Daffy Duck as she walked down the steps. She saw Helen and immediately ran over and wrapped her arms around her.

"I'm so glad to see you, Gigi," Lilly exclaimed. She saw Jesse and grabbed onto him, too. "Grandpa!" She beamed exuberantly.

Jesse spotted a mark on her cheek. "Oh, honey, how did you get that bruise?"

"I fell," she said quickly. "I'm a klutz." She laughed and brushed off the comment and turned to hug Lucas.

"Hi, princess." He grinned at her.

"Stop calling me princess!"

Lucas snickered at his friend. He enjoyed annoying her even more than he thought he would. "We're going back to Jake's house, and you'll meet Mama G and Jake," Lucas told her eagerly.

"So, I get to meet your second bestest friend? I looked it up, Lukie; you can have two best friends. I just get to be the ultimate best friend." She laughed.

"You and your Lillyisms," Lucas chuckled.

"I'm so excited to be here," Lilly beamed. "I can't wait to meet Mama G and Jake." Lilly loved anyone who gave her a chance.

"Oh, Mama G's going to love you," Jesse said. "She doesn't have a little girl around."

"Is she nice?"

"Oh, she's great. You'll like her."

"Cool." She grinned and held on to her Daffy doll.

When they reached Jake's house, Lilly walked up to the front door, holding her doll close to her, and a lady answered the door.

"Hi, Lilly. My name is Elizabeth. Come on in!"

"Hi," Lilly said shyly and took a hesitant step into the entryway.

"You are such a pretty little girl."

Lilly blushed. Lucas and Jacob giggled at her.

"This is my son, Jacob. Jacob, get over here right now!"

Jacob, unenthused, walked over to meet Lucas's other best friend. While he'd never noticed girls before—they had cooties—he did look at Lilly a little differently than he normally would.

"You boys take Lilly and play. You behave, Jacob Isaac! She's a guest in our house!"

"Oh, Mom, we don't want to play with no girls," he snarled.

"*Any* girls, and she's a guest. You treat her right," Elizabeth demanded.

"FINE!" Jacob grumbled and walked away.

"Come on, let's go play *Star Wars*." Lucas ran out to play.

"I ain't playing with a girl!"

"Come on. She's a cool girl!"

"I don't care!" Jacob walked up to Lilly and pulled her pigtails.

Lilly yelled and swatted his hands away. "I'm telling!" she warned then ran back into the house, assumedly to tell Elizabeth.

"See, she's a brat! She's gonna tell on me for pulling her pigtails."

"Man, you didn't have to do that."

"I'm not playing with no girls!"

Lucas looked at him in exasperation as Lilly came back out.

"Gigi told me to play with you."

"I'm not playing with no girl!" Jacob continued and pushed her to the side, knocking her down.

"Jake, man, stop it! You okay, princess?"

"Stop calling me princess!" Lilly stormed off and hid behind a tree.

"Jake, she's my friend. Don't be so mean to her."

"How can she be your friend and you be my friend? You have to pick one of us!"

"Look, man. I don't have to pick between you. I like both of you. You're both my friends. I've known Lilly since my mom died."

"Yeah, and you've known me since the laundromat, too."

"I know, but you don't have to pull her pigtails. It's not nice, man."

"What? Do you LIKE her?"

Lucas was quiet.

"YOU DO LIKE HER!" Jacob roared with laughter. "Lucas has a girlfriend, Lucas has a girlfriend," he sang, taunting him.

"Why are you being such a jerk?"

"Because you have a girlfriend." He chuckled.

Lucas did something he never did. He hauled off and decked Jacob, knocking his glasses off his head. "She's not my girlfriend! She's a girl who is a friend."

Jacob picked up his glasses and gave Lucas a hard shove. "She is your girlfriend," Jacob teased him more, and Lucas pushed him back.

They got into a roughhousing match, and Jesse came out of the house and broke them up.

"Behave, both of you! Or no TV for a week!"

"But Grandpa!" Lucas whined.

"I mean it! You two behave! Now, go back to playing, and be nice to Lilly. She's a guest, and we treat guests with what?"

"Respect," they mumbled in unison.

"Exactly! Now, go on and play." Jesse turned around and went back in the house without another word.

"Thanks," Jacob whined. "Now I'm going to hear about it from Mom."

"Oh, you started it! You don't have to be mean to her."

"But, Lu, she's a girl! Remember, we don't have girls in our club!"

"She can be Princess Leia!"

"She probably hasn't even seen the movies."

"We can watch them together, the three of us," Lucas told him. "I'm not doing anything with her," he huffed.

"Well, you're going to have to because she's here for the summer."

"Great, just great," Jacob said, annoyed at the new feelings he had for the girl with the blond pigtails.

"She's not that bad, Jake. Just give her a chance. She's a nice girl. You might like her."

"I don't want no stinking girlfriend!"

"You don't have to have her as your girlfriend, but you can be nice to her."

"You be nice to her. You're her Lukie," he snickered. "*Lukie! Lukie! Lukie!*"

"You better shut your damn mouth before I knock your teeth out, too!"

"*Lukie! Lukie! Lukie!*" He taunted him more.

Lucas went after him, and they got into another fight.

This time, Elizabeth came out, furious. "Jacob Isaac! If you two don't behave, I'm going to take a belt to both of your hides, and you won't be able to sit down for a week! Now behave!" Elizabeth fumed, turned around, and returned to the house, letting the door slam behind her.

"I just don't want to lose you, man. You're my friend, my only friend."

"You're not going to lose me, man. You're my best friend, too."

"I thought she was?" Jacob asked.

"You know it's possible to have two best friends, right?" Lucas reminded him.

"I guess," he snickered. They both noticed Lilly sitting out by a tree. "Hey, princess!" Jacob called.

Lilly innocently turned around, and Jacob picked up a mud ball and threw it at her. It landed right in her face, getting mud all over her hair.

"Stop calling me princess!" she screamed.

Jacob laughed, and he and Lucas ran off to play with their lightsabers.

Even after a couple of days, Jacob still didn't want anything to do with Lilly. *I don't like her!* he thought. *She's rich! She's got good clothes and lives in a big house. She's too good for me. I wear glasses and old clothes. I'm not good enough for her. But I can't help it; she gets me going. Those pigtails ... I just ... her hair smells like strawberries ... and her smile. Keep it together, Glass.*

Lilly wiped the tears from her eyes and held her knees close to her chest as she sat behind a tall oak tree, playing with her doll. This was not the summer she hoped to have. With Jacob pulling her pigtails all the time and Lucas telling him off, she felt even more alone. Being an only child, she was used to being alone for long periods of time, but it still hurt. She missed Lucas. She missed having their time together.

Lucas had a hard time as well, being caught in the middle. *Why is Jacob being such a jerk? Why is Lilly so sad? This is so frustrating! They should be getting along! They're my best friends, but they hate each other!* Lucas pondered and scratched his head in frustration.

"She's boring," Jacob complained. "Look at her, playing with her doll and the pebbles on the ground."

"She's my friend, Jake."

"Watch this," he snickered to Lucas.

"Jake, don't do anything, man. She's not hurting anyone. You're just being a jerk."

"There she is! Hey, *princess*." Jacob threw mud at her, but when she didn't turn around or act like it affected her in any way, he was disappointed she hadn't taken the bait. "Oh, come on, princess. Are you just going to stand there? You're no fun! Lucas is right; you're a drag."

Lilly glanced at Lucas as Jacob ran off.

"WHAT!? I never said that!!" Lucas huffed, then quietened. "I like you, Lilly. I like you a lot!"

"It's okay, Lukie," Lilly said softly, her voice reflecting the hurt she felt. "I know I'm not wanted."

"I want you here! I'm going to talk to Jake. I'll be right back." *I'm going to give him a piece of my damn mind!* Lucas thought as he stomped over to Jacob. "Man, why did you tell her that? I never said that to you at all! I like Lilly. She's a nice girl, once you get to know her."

"She's a stuck-up, snobby princess ... *Lukie*," he snickered at him.

"Don't you dare call me Lukie!" he said and then shoved Jacob.

"Lukie! Lukie! Lukie!" Jacob taunted him.

Lucas pulled his arm back to punch him, but Elizabeth was suddenly there and caught him in the act. "Lucas James Ashton, you stop right there!"

"But, Mama G!" Lucas pleaded.

"Don't Mama G me. I saw what was going on."

"He's being mean to Lilly," Lucas defended himself.

"Jacob Isaac, why are you being mean to that little girl? She's a sweet little girl."

"She's a stuck-up bitch, is what she is."

That did it. Elizabeth took Jacob's hand, marched him into the house, got a belt from her room, and spanked him. "You know we don't talk like that in this house!" She grabbed onto Jacob's hand as he spun around in circles, trying to get away from her spanking. "You apologize for calling that sweet girl that."

"Okay! Okay! I'm sorry," he sobbed. After about five whacks with a belt, she let him go.

"Now you go sit down and think about what you did while I get dinner ready."

"What about Lucas? He was going to deck me!"

"You want more than you just got? He was sticking up for her."

"What is the big deal with her? Why does everyone bow down to Lilly? She's nothing special!"

"Jacob Isaac!" Elizabeth went for the belt again.

"I'm sorry! I'm sorry!" he backed up, and Elizabeth stood down.

"Go wash up for dinner. You and Lucas both."

Once it got quiet in the house, Lilly came in and joined Elizabeth in the kitchen. "I can help you cook if you like, Mrs. Glass," Lilly offered.

Elizabeth smiled at her innocence. "Oh, honey, let's get you cleaned up. Jake and his mud. I'm sorry about that boy. He doesn't need to be throwing mud at you."

"It's okay," she sighed. "I'm used to not being wanted."

"Who doesn't want you?"

"My mom doesn't want me. I haven't seen her since I was six years old."

"Honey," Elizabeth bent down to Lilly's level. "I want you! I love you. You're a sweet little girl."

Elizabeth wrapped her arms around her, and Lilly held on tightly.

"I wish Jake liked me."

"I think Jake likes you. He just doesn't know how to show it. Come on, let's get you cleaned up." Elizabeth took Lilly into the bathroom and washed her up. "So, you like to cook?"

"Yeah, Miss Sarah is teaching me how to cook. I like to cook spaghetti."

"Do you?"

"Yeah," Lilly beamed. She was growing to love Mama G. "Well, good. That's what we'll have for dinner tonight." Elizabeth grinned and gently booped Lilly's nose. "Now," she led Lilly back into the kitchen, "here's an apron for you." Lilly took the old apron and copied Elizabeth as she put hers on. "Let's get a piece of paper, and I'll give you my secret recipe for my spaghetti sauce. You make this, and you'll have everyone loving your cooking." She grinned at the little girl. Lilly got a pen and paper and started writing.

A few days later, Lilly talked Elizabeth into taking her to work at the laundromat and then the restaurant. Lilly helped bus tables and swept floors, and Elizabeth gave her a couple of dollars for all her help. Elizabeth felt safe to her, and, for the first time in a long time, Lilly didn't feel alone. Jacob and Lucas had each other, but Lilly wanted someone in her corner. When Lilly asked Jesse to take her to the store, she spied the item she wanted right away. *Yes! I have enough to get it!* She couldn't wait to show Mama G.

Elizabeth sighed as she sat down, exhausted from a very long day of work. She wished she had the money to just order pizza, as she didn't feel like cooking anything. Matthew had sent some money to Helen to help take care of Lilly, and Helen had given it to Elizabeth since she would be taking care of her the most. But Elizabeth didn't feel comfortable spending it on frivolous things. *Better not squander the money. Thank you, Lord, for the blessing,* she prayed as she lay back against the wall still in her pink and white waitress uniform, her legs spread out across the floor. *Oh, peace and quiet!* She had just closed her eyes when a tiny, sweet, feminine southern voice spoke up.

"Mama G," Lilly whispered.

Elizabeth chuckled and looked at her. "Yes, baby."

"I have something for you," Lilly beamed.

"You have something for me?" Elizabeth asked, confused.

"Yeah, you gave me some money for helping you. I used it to get you something. I hope you like it." Lilly handed her a package. "I wrapped it in blue since that's my favorite color. What's your favorite color?"

"Purple. I love purple."

"The red purple or the blue purple?"

"Oh, the blue-purple, definitely. It's so dark and deep and rich. I just love it."

"I love blue. It's so rich, vibrant, and beautiful. It makes me smile."

"I like seeing you smile, baby." Elizabeth put her hand gently on Lilly's cheek. *She always flinches when I get too close.* "Let's see what you got me." She took the sparkly blue bow off.

"I hope you like it."

"I'm sure I'll love it whatever it is." Elizabeth unwrapped the paper to unveil a white apron with a screen-printed image on the front. It read "Kiss the Cook" and had a woman with blond hair and blue eyes who was holding a spoon and a giant cooking pot. It also had a giant, red kiss mark at the top. "Oh, Lilly," she chuckled. "This is so sweet."

"You like it?" Lilly was elated that she'd finally done something good.

"Like it? I love it! Thank you." Elizabeth hugged Lilly.

"I heard you say you needed a new apron."

"Baby, you didn't have to take your hard-earned money and buy me anything. You earned that."

"I know, but I wanted to do it for you. I love you, Mama G." She wrapped her arms around Elizabeth and laid her head against her stomach.

"I love you too, baby." Elizabeth kissed her head. "I love you, sweet girl. Now we have to get you one. I tell you what; I can show you how to make your own."

"You're going to teach me how to sew like you?"

"Yes, I will. After dinner tonight, we can sew you a little apron. I tell you what; we'll even go to the store and pick out the fabric you want."

"Can I get sparkly blue fabric?"

"Absolutely, baby. We'll get whatever you like."

"I'm so excited!" Lilly giggled, clapped her hands, and bounced on her tiptoes.

"Okay, let's get started on dinner." Elizabeth put her apron on and got the pans down. "Tonight, I'm going to teach you the way to Jake's heart."

"I don't want Jake's heart." Lilly giggled and wrinkled her nose.

"Someday, baby, you may want Jake's heart," she giggled.

The next day, the kids were at Jacob's house, and Jacob was back to his usual behavior. Before Lucas could stop him, Jacob threw mud at Lilly and got it in her hair.

"Jake, you have to stop tormenting her. She's my friend. She's my sister. If you don't stop tormenting her, I'm going to stop being friends with you."

"Lu! You can't stop being friends with me."

"Well, I can't take being in the middle anymore. You treat Lilly with respect, or I'm going home and you won't see me ever again. No more comics, no more playing or anything."

"FINE! Stupid *princess*," Jacob grumbled.

Elizabeth once again overheard him and took a belt to her son. Jacob ran into his room, screaming and growling. "I hate that stupid bitch!" Elizabeth went charging in. "What did you say?"

"I hate her! I want my mom and my friend back."

"You just stay in here and think about what you've done!" Elizabeth slammed the door, exasperated.

Jacob was frustrated and angry. He had no idea how to channel his new emotions and couldn't stop thinking about Lilly. *Her pigtails are so cute and her smile, with her dimples. God, Glass, what's wrong with you? Her giggle. Stay strong man. Don't get attached. She's leaving at the end of the summer. You'll never see her again. You'll never be good enough for her. She's a stuck-up bitch. I'll stop throwing mud. That's not very nice. She's going to have Lucas all to herself, and I'm going to be alone.* Jacob was somber at the thought.

Jacob sat in his room for a while until he got bored. He needed to see Lilly, to get those crazy feelings again. *She should be out of the shower now and smelling like strawberries.* Jacob went into the kitchen and found Lilly sitting in a chair at the table.

"Here, let me comb your hair for you," Elizabeth said to Lilly, then parted her hair down the middle and put it into two pigtail braids. "I do this so it doesn't get knotted up in between combings. You have the prettiest hair. It's so soft and silky. You have a peaches and cream complexion."

"Peaches." Jacob sniggered from behind her. "Princess Peach." Jacob laughed and pulled her pigtails.

Lilly cried. She'd had enough.

"Jacob, I told you do not be mean to Lilly."

"Oh, Mom, I'm just playing. Princess Peach knows that." Jacob looked at Lilly and smiled. *Strawberries.*

When Elizabeth finished, Lilly sat on the couch and held Daffy Duck. She carried Daffy around wherever she went. Daffy was her friend.

Jacob came by, "Daffy Duck!" He laughed, snatched Daffy from her hands, and threw it across the room. Lilly jumped on Jacob.

"My Uncle John got that for me! How dare you throw Daffy, you useless piece of shit! You can throw mud at me and pull my pigtails, but DAFFY DUCK IS OFF LIMITS! You stupid piece of shit!!" Lilly screamed at Jacob. Elizabeth ran to the living room and pulled Lilly off Jacob.

Lilly grabbed Daffy and ran into the closet. She sat on the floor under the hanging clothes and cried. "I'm so sorry, Daffy." She held the stuffed doll and cried.

Lucas knocked on the closet door, "Hey, Lilly, are you okay?"

"Why do you care; you hate me now? You got that stupid Jacob kid as your friend. You don't like me anymore."

"Lilly, you're still my friend."

She opened the door and let Lucas come in, then shut the door again.

"He doesn't like me. I wish I didn't have to stay here."

"Lilly, come out here," Elizabeth called to her.

"She's going to spank me now. I want to go home!" Lilly cried.

"You better go out there. Maybe it won't be as bad if you listen to her."

Lilly took Lucas's advice and opened the door cautiously. Elizabeth was standing there with a contrite-looking Jacob.

"What do you have to say to each other?" Elizabeth spoke to both of them.

"I'm sorry I threw your Daffy across the room."

"I'm sorry I punched you."

"Now hug it out," Elizabeth told them. At first, Jacob balked, but then Elizabeth added, "Do you want another spanking?"

"No." Jacob hugged Lilly. Elizabeth went to the kitchen and returned a towel with some ice.

"Here, this will help your eye. Somehow we have to get you new glasses now."

"I'm sorry, Mama G. I didn't mean to ruin his glasses," Lilly apologized.

"It's okay, Lilly. I understand."

"If you tell Daddy, he might get him a new set."

"No, your dad already sent some money. I'm going to use some of it and get his glasses fixed."

"I really am sorry."

"It's okay, baby. Jacob had it coming."

"But, Mom! She hit me!"

"Jacob Isaac!" Elizabeth looked at him sternly. "Now, you guys behave. I have to go to work now. I'm going to leave you three here alone. Lock the door and don't let anyone else in. I'll be home in about four hours. Don't stay up late. Lilly, you can sleep in my room. You boys can have Jacob's room. I love you. You behave."

Jacob sneered at Lilly, and she was immediately on high alert.

Lucas was once again caught in the middle. "Come on, guys! You had your fight. Jake, you promised you wouldn't treat her badly any more."

"He threw my Daffy," Lilly said in a low growl. "The Daffy Uncle John got me when Melinda left me."

"Who's Melinda?" Jacob asked.

"She's no one." Lilly sat there in a huff, trying not to cry. Daffy brought her comfort.

"Melinda is her mother," Lucas told Jacob. "She left her at her Uncle John's one weekend and never came back."

Jacob stared at Lilly. "I'm sorry Princess Peach. I didn't know."

Lilly wiped her face and bit her lip but said nothing.

"At least you know your mom. I never met my dad. He left before I was even born." Jacob told her.

"You've never met your dad?" Lilly turned to face Jacob.

"No. Once he found out about me, he took off. That's fine; I don't need him. I hope he falls off the face of the earth."

"And then there's me, who doesn't have either one," Lucas joked, but his voice dripped with sadness. "I'm the kid whose mother screwed up and died of drugs right by my crib. Why did she have to do that? Why did she have to die?" Lucas hurled a pillow across the room and broke a glass. "Oh, just great, just great," Lucas whined. He got a broom and swept it up. "I guess this makes us a special club. The screwed up kids' club."

"Yeah, all three of us have screwed up lives," Lilly admitted.

"You live in a huge house, though. You don't have to worry about food. You get to go anywhere in the world. You don't have to worry about anything."

Lilly looked down, ashamed. "I only go where they push me off to. No one at home wants me. I like it here. Mama G likes having me around, and she teaches me things. She's nice to me. I'd give up everything to have that, Jake. You have a great mom. You have something we don't have. So why do you behave so badly?"

"I don't know," Jacob grumbled. "I just get so frustrated at things. Things are happening to me, and I don't know what to do."

"What's going on?" Lilly asked.

"I like you a lot," Jacob confessed. "I like your pigtails." He reached over and gave them a light tug; Lilly swatted his hand away.

"Jake, do you like, like her?" Lucas asked.

"Yes," he admitted shyly.

"I like you too. I think you're cute," Lilly admitted shyly and reddened.

"You do?"

"Yeah. I like your blue eyes. You have the prettiest eyes."

"I do?" Jacob turned pink.

"Yeah." She smiled.

Jacob grinned and took her hand. "Princess Peach, you wanna watch our movies with us?"

"I'd love to."

From then on, the three of them were best friends. As summer started winding down, things between Jacob and Lilly had changed. They were boyfriend and girlfriend. He held her hand all the time, and they sat out by Lilly's tree together.

"You want to kiss?" Jacob asked bravely.

"You want to kiss me?" Lilly asked, surprised.

"I've never kissed a girl before," Jacob admitted.

Lilly's face turned various shades of pink. "I would like to kiss you. We do this J, we take it to the grave!"

"Pinky swear?" Jacob held out his little finger.

"Pinky swear!" Lilly stuck hers out and they clasped tightly.

Lilly grew shy and brushed a stray hair away from her face. Jacob took a deep breath and leaned over, as Lilly closed her eyes and puckered her lips. Jacob closed his eyes and clumsily met her lips with his own. They looked at each other afterward and giggled shyly.

"What did you think?" Jacob asked, his blue eyes looking at her through his new glasses.

Lilly's face flushed as she shyly giggled and kissed him again.

"I like this, Princess Peach!" Jacob wrapped his arm around Lilly. She laid her head on his shoulder, holding his hand in hers.

"I don't want this summer to end," Lilly admitted. "This has been the best summer of my life."

"Mine, too, princess. Mine, too."

"Will I always be your princess?"

"Will I always be your J?"

"There will be no other J for me."

"You're the only princess I want."

"I love you, Jacob Glass."

"I love you, too, Lilly Patrick."

"I hope we can come to see you sometime," Jacob admitted.

"I hope when I get big, I can come back here and see you and Mama G."

"I'd like that. You'll always be my Princess Peach."

"You'll always be my J."

No one wanted this summer to end, but it was time. Lilly said her goodbyes and walked over to the steps of the plane with Helen and Jesse to wait for Lucas.

He held onto Elizabeth for a long time.

"I'm going to miss you, Lulu, so much. You behave for me, okay? You take good care of yourself and get good grades. You watch out for Lilly. You are always welcome in this house; I want you to know that. No matter what happens, you are welcome in this house. You'll always be my son, no matter how old you get." Elizabeth tried to remain strong, but tears flowed down her cheeks. "I love you, Lulu."

"I love you too, Mama G. Please don't ever forget me," he pleaded.

"I'll never forget you at all, Lucas James. When the world gets too hard, you remember me and look at that star. I will always be thinking about you. Remember what I taught you. Say your prayers and read your Bible. Let God guide your path in every situation, and you will go far. You're a strong boy. You will succeed in whatever you set your mind to. I love you." She kissed his head, pulled him into a final embrace, and let him go. It was time to say goodbye to his best friend and his brother.

"I'll always remember you," Lucas said, trying to be strong.

"I'll always remember you, too. Remember our code."

"I'll always remember our code." Lucas hugged Jacob and handed him a bag of comics he'd brought with him. "Here's all of my best Avengers comics."

"Lucas, you didn't have to do that." Jacob was shocked.

"I wanted you to have something to remember me by."

"I'll never forget you, man. You're my best friend." He gave him a huge hug.

"And you're mine."

"Lucas," Helen said. "It's time." Lucas turned and waved at the top of the stairs and followed the others as they took their seats on the plane. Lilly was sobbing, and Jesse tried to soothe her.

"Hey, at least you have Lucas with you this time, bug."

Lilly smiled shyly at Jesse. "Yeah, I know," she said softly.

"I know it hurts, guys, but it was for the best. You might not see it now, but, in time, you'll see it. We get back, we'll get you settled in, and things will be back to normal in no time."

"We got this, princess. You know us; where there's one ..." He held out his hand for her to finish.

"There's the other," she said tenderly and smiled.

"We got each other. We can tackle anything." Lucas wrapped his arm around her. "It's princess and Lukie against the world."

Chapter Nine

Lucas squirmed and grumbled. He tugged at his tie and unbuttoned his jacket. "Why do I always have to wear a suit? It's hot! Why can't I wear shorts like I used to?" he protested to Jesse.

"You know, Matthew has important people over all the time, and we have to always look our best."

"It's itchy and chokes me," Lucas whined.

"It's just part of the rules, little man."

"Well, it's stupid! I have to wear this to school now?"

"Yeah, you'll have a uniform to wear. You'll look like a little businessman."

"What does a businessman do?"

"They run massive corporations. Just like you like to buy up properties in Monopoly."

"Yeah?"

"He buys up properties real cheap and develops them with businesses and sells them for high profit."

"What does he do with the profit?"

"He puts it back into his business and builds up more properties. He buys the horses and trains them to run, then he takes his winnings and puts them back into the business. It's a constant flow. He likes you. He thinks you would be a good businessman. He said he'd like to teach you how to run a business like this."

"Are we still going to see Uncle John and Aunt Sheryl on the weekends?"

"Yeah, I'll still take you up there. He's excited that you're moving down here. He's excited to see his Jughead again."

"Jughead." Lucas chuckled. "I don't think he even knows what my name is."

"He loves you. He likes to tease you."

"I love Uncle John. He's like a dad to me."

"Yeah, he's a good guy. Here, let me show you how to straighten that up." Jesse undid Lucas's tie and showed him how to tie it so it wasn't so tight on his throat.

"I still don't see why I have to wear these things," Lucas grumbled.

"I know, little man; I know."

A couple of days later Matthew sat in his lavish office. He was busy at work when Lucas came in.

"You wanted to see me?" Lucas said.

"Yes." Matthew walked over to an armchair, where he motioned for Lucas to sit. "Let me teach you the art of the deal."

Matthew put the phone on a conference call and spoke with other delegates across the country. "I have Lucas in here. He's like a son to me. I'm taking him under my wing. Say hi, Lucas."

"Hi," Lucas said.

"Hi," the chorus came from people on the call.

"Now, where were we?"

When Matthew continued with the call, Lucas listened intently. A few minutes later, Matthew wrapped up his call.

"So, are you buying that apartment complex?" Lucas asked.

"Yes. It's run down and dilapidated. We're going to tear them down and build a high-rise tower where people can live."

"What about the people that live there now?"

"Well, this one no one lives in. If someone lived there, we'd make them a fair offer so they could move to a different place. You see, son, the trick is to buy when it's really low and then sell it when it's high."

"How do you know when it's real high?"

"You follow the stock market."

"Is that where everyone screams at the camera and that thing goes across the screen?"

"Yes," Matthew chuckled, "the ticker. The stock market opens, and people trade and sell stocks. You have it in you, Lucas. I've seen it since you were a little boy. You stick with me, son, and you'll have a house ten times the size of this place and have more money than you'd ever be able to spend. Whatever you do, don't let anyone take you for granted. You stay true to yourself and never take no for an answer. If you want something, you get it at all costs. That's the cost of business. Now ..." he opened a drawer, "I was told how good you are at this."

"Oh, yeah! I love Monopoly!" Lucas was excited.

"I heard you're a prodigy at it. If you can beat me, I'll let you wear your regular clothes for a week."

He smiled at him. "No suit, no tie. One thing about business, Lucas, you always must look professional. You must always look your best. No one can see your vulnerable side. If they see your vulnerable side, then they will use it against you and tear you down. Always remain strong and tough. That's the only way you'll succeed."

"So, if I can beat you, I can wear normal clothes for two weeks." Lucas smiled.

"One week." Matthew chuckled.

"A week and a half?"

"Three days," Matthew countered.

"Okay, one week," Lucas conceded.

"Good boy." Matthew opened the box and put the board on the table. "I'm setting my watch for one hour. At the end of one hour, whoever has the most money is the winner. Shake on it." He reached his hand out. Lucas, feeling confident, shook his hand and rolled the dice.

At the end of one hour, Lucas realized he had met his match when it came to Matthew. "A suit and tie it is," he conceded.

After school on Friday, Jesse took Lucas and Lilly to see John. "Don't forget to get Uncle John his sandwich," Lilly reminded Jesse. "We forgot his milkshake last time."

"Can I get some chocolate fudge?" Lucas asked.

"Oh, yes, please. They have the good peanut butter fudge." Lilly said.

"Yeah, we'll stop and get the fudge and a milkshake." Jesse chuckled as he drove the kids to Uncle John's house, with one important stop.

Soon Lilly spied the fifties-themed diner up ahead. "Look, Grandpa! There it is! It's so cute!" The restaurant was inside a metal mobile home with a neon sign that read *Rosie's* in retro green and pink colors with a neon flamingo on top. Green and pink neon designs were all over the building. It was tacky, but, to Lilly, it was cute. "I love the flamingo," she giggled. "I want a flamingo burger, now that I know they're not made with real flamingos."

"I can't believe you believed Joe when he told you that." Lucas laughed. "Where do flamingos even live?" Lucas asked. Jesse sighed because he knew what was coming, a Lillyism on flamingos.

"I got curious, and I looked them up. I missed going to the library when I was in New York. I have a whole list of things I have to look up, now that I'm back home."

"You and your Lillyisms." Lucas laughed.

When Lucas stepped up to order, he took notice of the cashier. *She's kinda cute! Long brown hair, hazel eyes. Hmm ... I like older women. Denise, what a lovely name. Denise and Lucas.* He giggled at the thought. "I'll have a flamingo burger, a chocolate shake, and flamingo fries," Lucas blurted out but then tried to recover by being cool. "How are you doing, Denise?" When Lucas started putting the moves on the cashier, Lilly laughed heartily because the cashier must have been around seventeen. Denise was patient and smiled at him, but she had a job to do. "I like older women," he smooth-talked her.

Jesse started laughing and pushed him out of the way. "Ignore him."

Lucas chuckled and went to the back of the line. When Denise handed the order to the cook, she looked at Lucas and winked at him. Lucas beamed his million-dollar bright smile.

"Lukie, she's too old for you." Lilly giggled.

"Hey, you miss a hundred percent of the shots you don't fire."

"Why would you have a shot and not fire it?" She looked at him, confused.

Lucas sighed and shook his head. "And I'm the Jughead?" He chuckled and drank his milkshake.

Lilly ran up the long walkway to John's house. She was excited to see him. She did a *rat-a-tat-tat* on the glass door and jumped up and down when he opened it.

"There's my Squirrel!" He opened his arms to her.

She beamed cheerfully as she wrapped her arms around his protruding belly and held on tight.

"Oh, Squirrel, it's so good to see you. It feels like I haven't seen you in forever."

"I went to New York this summer."

"I know! I missed you so much." John smiled.

"I missed you, too." She kissed him on the cheek. John stepped aside and let her in to see his kids sixteen year old Joe and ten year old Mary. John then hugged Helen and Jesse.

"Oh, Dad, I'm so glad you're living so close now. How are you doing?"

"We're doing well. How's Sheryl?"

"They're testing her for leukemia."

"Oh, John," Jesse whispered.

"They're not sure what's going on with her. She can't keep any iron in her, and she keeps bleeding profusely."

"Oh, son," Jesse breathed.

"Yeah, so we're having a hard time right now. But I'm so glad you guys came. I needed to see you guys. I need my family," John admitted.

"Yes, son, of course," Jesse wrapped his arms around John, "I'll always be here for you."

"I love you, Dad." John hugged him tightly.

"I love you, too."

John let go of Jesse and smiled down at Lucas. "There's my Jughead!" He laughed. "Boy, you are getting so big! I missed you this summer."

"I missed you too."

"How are you doing in school?"

"Well, Angie Johnson has PE with me, so I'm excited." He laughed and John roared.

"Oh, Jug, you're something else. Come on, guys, let's go eat." He led them into the kitchen.

Sheryl held onto the kitchen table. Her face was as white as snow. "Hi, Lucas. I'm so glad to see you. I missed you." She opened her arms up to him, and Lucas hugged her. She held onto him to keep from stumbling over.

"You okay, Aunt Sheryl?"

"Yeah, I ... I don't feel good, honey. I'll be okay, though, but I'm going to go lie down. You guys keep it down, okay?"

"Okay, Aunt Sheryl." Lucas watched as Sheryl walked slowly back towards her bedroom, then gave his Uncle John a concerned look. "Is she going to be okay?"

"She needs all the prayers she can get, Jug. She's not feeling too well. So, you guys have to be good, okay?"

"I understand." Lucas looked at him.

"Thanks, Jug." John squeezed his shoulder.

On Saturday evening, Joe's band, Echo, had a show at the local high school. Joe was excited because they had practiced hard and had a set list of the top rock songs from some of his heroes. "We even wrote a couple songs we're going to play tonight," he told Lucas. "I hope it goes well, man."

"It will. You guys are great. You'll have all the girls after you."

"Can't go wrong with that." Joe laughed and high-fived Lucas.

A little while later they were loading up the equipment and making their way over to the school. The other members of Echo set up their gear and got ready while Gina, Joe's girlfriend, did Joe's makeup.

Lucas laughed at how silly he looked, but Joe loved it. Lilly, Lucas, Gina, and Mary stood at the side of the stage and watched Echo rock the house.

Lucas looked around at the girls screaming and dancing. They loved Joe. "Look at those girls! They're screaming for Joe!" Lucas thought that was the funniest thing in the world. Overall, the kids had a great time. Joe felt the energy and the fire. He was hooked.

After church on Sunday, Lilly got emotional because she didn't want to go home.

Aunt Sheryl hugged her and said, "You be a good girl, Punky, and I'll see you next weekend."

"I will, Aunt Sheryl. You get better." She held onto her dear aunt.

"I will. God's going to take care of me." Sheryl smiled at Lilly.

Then—the part that was the hardest—Lilly went over and wrapped her arms around Uncle John.

"Squirrel, you don't have to cry. You'll see me next weekend."

"I know, but what if I can't come up next weekend?"

"I'll come and get you. We always spend the weekends together."

"I know, but I miss you during the week."

"You know you can call me anytime."

"I can?"

"Why, yes, of course. I love hearing from you."

"I love you, Uncle John." Lilly hugged him.

"I love you, too." He smiled and kissed her head.

"It's time to go, Lilly," Jesse told her. Lilly let go of John and grabbed her Daffy doll, took Jesse's hand, and walked out the door. She turned around and looked back at the family that loved her so much, then waved goodbye and made her way to the truck to go back home.

Chapter Ten

Lucas had been in Kentucky for a month. He adapted well and was accustomed to his routine, and, after many tries, he finally won a game of Monopoly against Matthew.

"I won!" he declared, clearly surprised.

But Matthew growled and glared at Lucas. He didn't like being bested at anything, much less to a little kid.

"I get to wear normal clothes for a week!"

"Three days," Matthew snarled.

"Huh?"

"Three days."

"No, you said a week!"

"I'm changing the terms of our deal. It's three days!"

"That's not fair! We've been playing every day for a month, and I finally win and you're changing the terms?"

"Did we sign a contract?"

"We shook on it!"

"Not a legally binding contract," Matthew groused.

"That's bullshit!"

Matthew backhanded Lucas across the face. Lucas stared at him in shock, straightened up, and slapped him back. Matthew didn't respond to the slap.

He'd been drinking after a bad day filled with losing deals, and any filters he normally had when sober had vanished. "Don't you swear at me, young man!" He hit him again.

"Don't hit me, old man!"

"Don't disrespect your elders!" He slapped him again; Lucas turned to leave. Then Matthew grabbed him by the arm and threw him across the room.

"What the hell?!"

"You're such a snot-nosed brat! Your mom was nothing but a whore!"

"Don't you start on my mom!" Lucas crossed the room and pummeled him with his fist, but Matthew pushed him away.

"You don't even know your mom and what kind of whore she was! Getting knocked up by a scumbag drug addict." Matthew kept taking swigs of his whiskey and wiping his mouth off with the back of his hand. "She was nothing but a drug addict! Had to bail her out myself, and what does she do? She shoots up. She dies right next to her son's crib and leaves me holding the bag." He slapped him again. "You're nothing but trash. Ugly drug-riddled trash." Matthew reached back and slapped Lucas again, knocking him to the ground. Then he started kicking Lucas in the stomach. Lucas pleaded with everything in him for Matthew to stop, but Matthew was too drunk and continued beating him.

"HELP!! HELP!!" Lucas screamed, but no one came. "HELP! GIGI!" Lucas screamed in pain.

JUST THE TWO OF US

Finally, the door opened, and Lilly ran in. "Oh, no!" Lilly gasped and ran over to Matthew. "Daddy! Please don't hurt him! Please! Whatever he did, he didn't mean it and won't do it again!"

"GO AWAY, YOU PIECE OF TRASH!" Matthew slapped Lilly.

Lilly looked at Lucas lying on the floor. Matthew resumed kicking him. She grabbed Matthew by the leg and held on. "Please, Daddy, hit me instead! Don't hurt Lucas! Please, Daddy, please!" she pleaded.

"Let go of my leg!" He went to kick Lucas, but with Lilly hanging on his leg, he slipped, kicking Lucas in the face. Two of Lucas's teeth went flying across the room, as Matthew lost his balance and fell backward onto the floor. Lilly let go of his leg and went over to Lucas in tears. Lucas looked at her, scared out of his mind.

"Come on, Lukie, hurry!" she urged him, while helping him up and pushing him towards the door. Lucas ran as fast as he could, with Lilly close behind—until Matthew grabbed her by the arm.

"You're sticking up for that brat?!!" He backhanded her, knocking out a tooth.

"Daddy, please don't hurt me!!" she pleaded, but he had an evil look in his eyes and kept drinking his whiskey.

"You're nothing but trash!" Lilly curled up on herself. She looked for an escape route but saw none. Then the door flew open.

"MATTHEW WILLIAM PATRICK!! What did you do!?" Jesse was livid at what he'd heard from the hallway.

"Get out of here, old man! And take your loser grandson with you!"

"Listen here, you son of a bitch! Hitting little kids! Pick on someone your own size! You think you're big enough?! Take me on!" Jesse got in his face and stood toe-to-toe with Matthew.

Matthew took a swing at Jesse, but Jesse easily caught his hand and threw him to the ground. "If I ever see you hitting these kids again,

I will wipe the floor with your ass!!" Jesse left Matthew to lie on the floor.

Lucas went to Miss Betty the maid. She gave him a solemn look and mumbled, "Oh, I hoped this wouldn't happen to you." She looked over his cuts and bruises. "I had hoped he was over his mad spells. I like you, Mr. Lucas. What did you do to have him do this?"

"I won a game of Monopoly."

"Oh, Mr. Lucas," Miss Betty said tenderly and put some antiseptic on his cut. "We'll have to get Dr. Aikman in here to look at your teeth."

"What did I do to have him do this? He's never done this to me before. I liked him. I thought he was nice." Lucas asked, confused and scared.

"You just have to be careful when he drinks," she admitted. "He had a bad day, and, when that happens, he drinks and then ..." she sighed, "he gets mean like this."

"He does this all the time?"

"Sadly, yes. I've had to stitch up Miss Lilly several times."

"Why doesn't anyone do anything to help?"

"We tried but several people have been fired for trying to help."

"Can't the cops do something?"

"He says he's disciplining her, and they go along with it."

"How often does it happen?"

"When he gets to drinking it happens. He has been sober for a while so we thought it was over." She sighed.

"He talked bad about my mom," Lucas groaned. "I don't know my mom."

"Don't let him get to you. Just be a good kid, and you'll be okay." She stitched the cut on his cheek.

"I try to be. I'll try to do better."

"You do that, Mr. Lucas. There. You're all fixed up now. Here's some Tylenol for the pain. Let me help you back to your room."

"Thank you, Miss Betty," he said as they went down the hall.

"I better check on Miss Lilly," Betty whispered and Lucas followed. They found Lilly lying on the bed in tears. Lucas went over to one side of the bed, and Betty went to the other. "Let me check you out, Miss Lilly."

Lilly looked at her with tear-stained cheeks. "Miss Betty, I thought I was a good girl now. I thought I was no longer trash, but it came back. How do I stop being trash? Can Dr. Cousins prescribe me something?"

"Miss Lilly, you're not trash, sweetheart."

"Daddy says I am when he hurts me." She looked at Lucas. "I'm so sorry, Lukie. I thought we wouldn't get hurt. I thought I was a good girl, and he stopped hurting. I was wrong, and now you're getting hurt, too," she sobbed. "I did everything I could. Please don't be mad at me."

"I'm not mad at you, Lilly."

"You're not?"

"No, you came to my defense. Are you okay?"

"Yeah, it only hurts for a little while."

"I have some medicine for you." Betty handed her a glass of water and some Tylenol.

"Thank you, Miss Betty."

"You're welcome, sweetheart." She sighed. "I'll have Dr. Aikman come check on the both of you tomorrow. I hope you guys get to feeling better." Betty left.

"Can I stay with you? I'm afraid to be alone," Lucas asked.

"Yes, I don't want to be alone. Dr. Aikman will be over after school to fix our teeth. You'll like him; he's nice. He doesn't hurt, either."

"Why doesn't he do something?"

"He heard about Dr. Van Pelt."

"Who's Dr. Van Pelt?"

"He was the old dentist. He tried reporting how I was always falling and busting my teeth. Someone came and asked me questions and spoke with Daddy. Dr. Van Pelt suddenly stopped coming around, and I saw on the news that his clinic caught on fire and everything was destroyed. I heard he moved to Virginia."

"That's some coincidence that his office caught on fire." Lucas raised an eyebrow.

"Daddy said the same thing."

"Lils, he had it done," Lucas informed her.

"Daddy wouldn't do that," Lilly got defensive.

"Lils."

"He wouldn't. That's arson. Daddy isn't an arsonist."

"No, he's just abusive," he grumbled. "But as long as he doesn't start fires," he said sarcastically.

"Don't talk bad about my dad." As abusive and hurtful as Matthew was, she still loved him. He was her daddy, after all.

"I'm sorry. How can you defend him?"

"Because he's all I have in the world, just like Gigi and Grandpa are all you have."

"Well, not anymore. I have you, and you have me."

"You mean that?"

"Of course!"

"Thanks, Lukie." She smiled, revealing a swollen gum where a tooth should have been. "Ow, it hurts to smile."

"It hurts to breathe," Lucas admitted. Lilly gave him some breathing techniques she'd discovered to deal with the pain.

The next day Lucas wore his street clothes to dinner.

"Why aren't you in your suit, young man?" Matthew got stern.

"Because you said I could wear my normal clothes since I won at Monopoly."

"Why didn't you come in for your lesson?"

"I didn't think you wanted me."

"You know the routine. You come in for your lesson after school. We play Monopoly, and then you do your homework." Matthew glared at him.

"Even after last night?"

"Last night was an unfortunate incident, and I apologize. The Workman merger went down the tubes, taking $1.2 million with it."

"What happened?"

"They backed out of the deal. They didn't want to sell because they got a better offer."

"But it was a fair offer for what you were getting."

"Very good, young man. I see you are learning from the lessons. Now go change into your suit. Wear your suit at dinner."

"But ..." Lucas protested.

"Lukie?" Lilly prodded. Lucas looked at her and groaned. He stormed back to his room and put on his black suit with a Spiderman tie. Matthew at least let him wear cool ties. Lucas resumed his seat at the table to find a guest had joined them.

"Lucas, this is Mrs. Joyner. She's with the Arizona Center for Athletics."

"Oh, yeah. I remember talking to you. You're looking for corporate sponsors for a new stadium."

"Yes, that's right. It's nice to meet you." Lucas shook her hand. "How is that going?"

"That's why I'm here. I'm seeing if we can get Patrick Industries on board with the new stadium."

"I thought I'd let Mr. Ashton here decide," Matthew explained. Lucas looked at him, surprised. "Mrs. Joyner is going to give you her proposal, then you think it over and decide if it's a good business deal. Whatever you decide, we'll go along with it."

Shock washed over Lucas. This was a tremendous opportunity. Over dinner, he listened to her proposal and liked what he heard, but something in his gut said it wasn't a good idea. "Matthew, can I speak to you in private?" Lucas asked.

Matthew took him to his office, and they had a discussion.

"It sounds like a good deal, but something isn't right. My gut says not to do it, and Mama G said to always go with your gut."

"You think it's a poor investment?"

"Yes, it just doesn't feel like a good opportunity. They only wanted to use the name for two years? What if it's not a successful team? Do you want to have your name associated with that? Something ... something isn't right. I can feel it."

"You're smarter than your years, young man. That is why I wanted you to decide. You are listening and paying attention to what I have taught you. I agree with your decision, but you get to give her the bad news."

"How do I do that?"

"You just be honest and upfront. It's nothing personal; it's just business. Remember that." Matthew gingerly put his hand on Lucas's shoulder, causing him to tense up.

"Yes, sir." Lucas followed him out of the office and back to the dinner table. He shook Mrs. Joyner's hand again and sat down. "After considering carefully, I will have to decline your offer, respectfully. I think at this time Patrick Industries' resources are better utilized elsewhere." Mrs. Joyner was noticeably upset but understood.

"You're letting a ten-year-old—" she started.

"Eleven," Lucas corrected her.

"... an eleven-year-old make your business decisions? I agree this isn't the best use of our mutual resources." Dinner was tense then Mrs. Joyner abruptly left.

"Did I make a mistake?" Lucas asked.

"You did the right thing, Lucas," Matthew told him. "How did it feel to make that decision?"

"Stressful, exhilarating, and powerful." He smiled brightly.

"Get used to it, young man. You're going to be making those decisions for the rest of your life." Matthew smiled at him. When he was sober, Matthew Patrick was a kind, generous man; however, when things didn't go well, he resorted to drinking and then to abuse. Matthew's father had been abusive from the time Matthew was six until his passing when Matthew was twelve. So, to Matthew, abuse was the only discipline he knew.

A couple of days later, Matthew took Lilly and Lucas out to the stables to show them some new horses he had bought. Lilly loved hanging out with the horses. She knew how to take care of them and was a splendid rider.

"This is a horse we got in today. Liliana, I'm going to let you name it."

"I get to name it?"

"Yes." He smiled.

"Cool!" Lilly clapped her hands excitedly.

"What are you going to name it?" Lucas asked.

"Well, I like the color blue," she thought aloud.

"Right."

"And I saw a show where they kept saying 'Isn't that wizard?'," she talked through her naming process.

"I like that show." Lucas chuckled.

"How about Blue Wizard?"

"Blue Wizard," Matthew repeated. "I like it. Blue Wizard."

The horse neighed and bobbed its head up and down. Lilly walked over to it. Blue Wizard reached over, sniffed her hair, and tried to take a bite of her pigtail. Lilly laughed and pulled her head away. "Don't eat me, Whizzy!" She laughed, but her eyes sparkled in excitement.

"This is another horse I got," Matthew pointed to the next stall, "His name is Crusader."

"Crusader! I like it," Lucas smiled.

Crusader was all black and had a small speckle of grey on his nose. "This can be your horse, Lucas."

"I get a horse?"

"Yes, every Patrick gets a horse."

"Cool! I get my own horse!" Lucas beamed.

"Let's take them out riding."

Matthew saddled the horses, and they rode the trail around the lake. Everyone enjoyed their afternoon ride with no thoughts about Matthew's abuse. That was the way life progressed. When Matthew had too much to drink, he'd take it out on the kids, and then the next day act like nothing ever happened.

It was now the weekend, and the kids were excited to go to Ashland, where they were safe, but their bruises from Matthew hadn't yet healed.

"Jug, what's wrong with your eye? Squirrel what happened to you?" John asked them as he welcomed him into the house.

"Billy Bates punched me."

"Why did he punch you?"

Lucas wasn't good at making up stories, as Elizabeth had always taught him to be honest and never lie. He looked at Lilly, who was better at it.

"Because he's a bully, and he doesn't like us," Lilly lied, explaining why both of them had bruises.

"Did you tell anyone?"

"It doesn't matter," Lucas growled. "Nothing's ever done."

"Well, when he hits you, hit him back."

"Like I never thought of that," Lucas said sarcastically.

"Jug," John scolded him.

"Sorry. I tried hitting him back, and it just made it worse."

"Well, I'm going to talk to that brother of mine and have him talk to the school. He can do something."

Lilly and Lucas looked at each other, scared.

"It won't matter, Uncle John. Something else will happen, no matter who we tell."

Lucas and Lilly hung out with Joe and Mary, leaving John and Jesse alone.

"He's hitting him just like Beau hit Matthew," John growled. Beau was John and Matthew's biological father.

"John, I handled it. There's an investigation—"

"That investigation isn't going anywhere! You don't know this, but I tried so many times to get custody of Lilly, and he always blocked it. That's why she went to New York for the summer. We had a hearing, and he didn't want her to know about it. He has the local judge in his back pocket. You better watch him, Dad, before something tragic happens."

"I know, son. I didn't know he was abusing her. I would have never moved down here if I knew, and now it's too late."

"He hurts her again, I'll come down there and beat the hell out of him myself! I'll show him what a real father does to someone that hurts his daughter!"

John looked at Lilly and Lucas, sitting together in the living room. They sat so close together, as if to protect each other, and they jumped at the littlest things. It was sad and sweet at the same time.

"Oh kids," John said softly and made sure to spend extra time with them over the weekend.

Chapter Eleven

It was now November, and things at home had been mostly okay for a while. Matthew was on a sober streak was rarely abusive. Lucas, however, liked a girl at school who wasn't paying him any attention. No matter what he did, she acted as if he wasn't worth the bother, and it drove him crazy! In a last-ditch effort to get her to say something, Lucas slapped her on the bum. She decked him, and Lucas was sent home. There was probably no good time for Matthew to deal with something like that, but he'd had another bad day and lost control from the moment he got home.

"So, you think it's okay to do that to little girls, huh?!"

Lucas said nothing.

"I'm talking to you, boy!" Matthew reeked of alcohol.

"No, I was just having fun."

"Having fun, huh? I'll show you having fun."

Matthew slapped Lucas across the face, and Lucas hit him back, which didn't faze Matthew in the least. He knocked Lucas to the floor and then kicked him in the stomach.

When Lilly heard the commotion, she ran to Lucas's defense. "Daddy, stop, please! Lucas didn't mean it! Please stop!"

"Get out of the way, Liliana!"

"But, Daddy, please!" she begged with her whole heart.

While Lucas lay in a fetal position in tears, Matthew pushed Lilly out of the way and continued to kick Lucas in the stomach. "You're a worthless brat! You think it's okay to do that to girls? I'll show you what a real man does, you hear!" Matthew kept kicking, while Lilly grabbed onto his leg, crying and begging him to stop. She held on for dear life. "You spoiled brat! Get out of here you piece of trash!" He punched and kicked Lilly, giving Lucas a reprieve.

"Don't hurt her!" Lucas yelled "Help!!! Someone help us!!!" Lucas yelled and punched Matthew's leg. Matthew started on Lucas again as Lilly lay there bleeding.

"Oh, you think someone will help you, little boy. No one is going to help you! I'm the father around here, and what I say goes!" Matthew kicked Lucas.

The door flung open, slamming against the wall. When Lucas saw her standing there, he knew they were saved. He scurried over to Lilly, and they crawled to a corner and held on to each other.

"MATTHEW WILLIAM PATRICK!!!" Deidre—Matthew's grandmother—spoke sternly and without fear. She stood a mere 5'3", but to Lilly and Lucas, she was a giant. She was their savior. No one messed with Mhamo Deidre.

"I just returned from a six-month trip to the homeland and find you hurting these kids again?! I told you to stop hurting them, and it looks like you didn't listen. This is MY HOUSE! These are my grandkids, and you WILL NOT hurt them! You hear me?" She stood her ground with her hands on her hips and dared him to say something.

"You old bitch!! You should die, too!" Matthew said as he took a swig of his whiskey. Deidre's eyes narrowed, and the intensity of her gaze sent a shiver throughout the room.

"That's what you think!!" She said firmly. She pulled the belt she had around her waist and slapped his ass. She didn't care how old he was—she was the mhamo and what she said went.

"You will not mistreat these kids like that!" Lucas and Lilly sat in the corner, shocked. Matthew tried to hit her which made her fury even stronger. "Don't think you're going to get the best of me, son!" After a few whacks, she stepped back. Matthew glared at her while she stood her ground. "You hurt those kids again, son, and you will get more of that!" She brushed the hair out of her face.

"I'll have you arrested!" Matthew shouted at her. Deidre stood with her hand on her hip.

"Try it, son! Just try it! You mess with me and you will be out on the street with no place to go! Now, Lucas," she kept her eyes on Matthew with the belt firmly in her hand and her other hand on her hip. "... call the cops. Matthew needs to spend a few nights in jail. Go on now." Lucas took Lilly's hand, and they raced out of the room.

"Now get up and straighten yourself out. You have a mug shot to take." Deidre put her belt back on and slammed the door as she walked out.

Matthew spent the night in jail. The next morning, he spoke with his friend Judge Everest.

"I was disciplining my son. You know how boys are at that age. Think they can get by with anything."

"I know, Mr. Patrick. I had to take care of my Charlie a few times. I'll sign off on the release, and we can enjoy that bottle of bourbon you brought me. I think we can both use a drink after this." Judge Everest signed the release papers, and the two of them sat back in chambers and spoke about their golf game and Matthew's donations to Judge Everest's political fund.

A couple of days later, John and his family came over for Thanksgiving. "What did you do to them?!!" John got in Matthew's face.

"I took care of it," Deidre interceded. "Now sit down and eat." Deidre clearly thought the matter was settled.

"I'm filing for custody of the both of them! They don't need to live here like this!"

"They're my kids!" Matthew said firmly. "I will do as I see fit!"

"Things have been handled. Now, we will finish dinner and have no more talk of it!!!" Deidre said sternly and slammed her fist down on the table. John opened his mouth, and Deidre narrowed her gaze on him. "I said no more! Now, pass the cranberry sauce, please."

After Thanksgiving dinner, Lilly and Lucas took a walk to the stables. Both of them were sore, but the fresh air felt good on their faces. "I'm sorry he started on you. I can take it, but I don't want you to get hurt." Lucas said.

"It hurts when he beats you. I can't stop it. It makes me cry harder. I should have begged them to not let you move down here. I don't want you to get hurt, Lukie. I love you. You're my best friend, and best friends love each other, according to Grandpa."

"I love you too, princess, and you're right; best friends love each other."

"You have got to stop acting out."

"I can't help it. Amanda ignores me, and I want her to like me."

"Lucas, there are other girls in school."

"Yeah, but they're not Amanda," he whined.

"Is she worth this, though?"

"Oh, be honest. If it wasn't this it would be something else."

"We have to do something so he doesn't hurt us anymore, Lukie. We have to pledge to each other."

"What can we pledge?"

"We will do everything in our power to behave and not get him upset. My stomach hurts, and I worry about you. If it was just me, I could take it. I've been doing it since I was six, but I have you now, and I don't want you to get hurt."

"He just makes me so angry!" Lucas curled his hands into fists by his side.

"We'll get through this, Lukie. We're … we're … we're wizards," she giggled and looked at Blue Wizard.

"No, we're Crusaders! Like my horse." Lucas smiled.

"Yeah, I like that! The Double L Crusaders!"

"Yeah, there you go! We're the Double L Crusaders, and I promise to protect you with all my heart at all times." He made a fist.

"I promise to protect you with all my heart at all times." Lilly made a fist, and they fist-bumped three times, high-fived three times, low-fived three times, and then slapped their hands side-by-side three times. "Our own little club. Just the two of us."

"Just the two of us."

Chapter Twelve

Later that evening, Deidre was watching a show about ballroom dancing on TV as Lucas walked by the den. "Come watch this with me. I like to watch them dance. It reminds me of being a girl in the homeland. I used to dance like this all the time. See them move. Look how confident they are. He's leading her around the room. It's like a fairy tale. You and Lilly can do this."

"I'm not a dancer, Mhamo."

"You can learn! Learn for your Mhamo. It gives you culture. Here dance with me." Deidre took Lucas's hand and showed him a few steps. Lucas realized he liked it. "You can be such a fine gentleman dancer. You learn to dance, Lucas, and you can get any girl you want."

"I can?" Lucas perked up.

"Yes, you can. You have grace and elegance. You will make a fine dancer. You can enroll in competitions and win money. You can buy all the comic books you want."

"I can win money?"

"Oh, yes. We sponsor many dance competitions. Do you think you can get Lilly to dance with you?"

"I'm her Lukie. She'll do anything for me." Lucas chuckled.

"Very well talk to her, and we'll get it set up," she said as they continued to dance around the room.

After the show, Lucas went to the indoor basketball gym. Lilly dribbled the ball and shot around. She was a phenomenal basketball player, and star of her team. "Hey, Lukie." She said as she shot the ball.

"I have a favor to ask. I need a partner, and I think you'd be good at it. Mhamo asked me to take dance lessons. She said I can get any girl I want by learning how to dance, and I need a partner."

"Lukie, I don't want to learn how to dance. I'm not good at it."

"How do you know? Have you ever tried?"

"I have two left feet."

"Please Lils?"

"Fine," she sighed.

"Thanks, Lils. I appreciate it."

A couple of days later, Lilly and Lucas walked into their first dance class. Lilly looked around at the group of students. "Lukie I don't know about this. They're so graceful, and I'm a klutz."

"You'll be fine."

"The things I let you talk me into."

"There will come a time when you'll talk me into something." Lucas chuckled. "Do this for your Crusader."

"There's nothing I wouldn't do for you, Lukie."

"There's nothing I won't do for you, either, Lilly." They took their places for their first lesson.

After several weeks of classes, their instructor, Mr. Dion, had them stay behind after class one day. "You guys are so good. You should enroll in the competition in Louisville at the end of the month."

"Oh, I'd love that! I'm super competitive," Lilly said. "You watch, Mr. Dion, I'm going to practice very hard and make you proud."

"I am proud of you, Miss Lilly and Mr. Lucas."

"I can't believe we get to perform in competitions," Lilly beamed.

"Do you think Gigi and Grandpa will come?"

"I hope so. Maybe Uncle John can come. Do you think Daddy will come?" Lilly asked, hopeful.

"No, he's not gone to any of the recitals," Lucas reminded her. "Still, Mhamo will be there. She loves going to our recitals."

"I'm glad she got us into this. I'm having fun. Okay, Lukie we got to go practice. I want to place first at competition!"

Lilly and Lucas spent many hours in the dance studio getting their routine just right. Lilly was a slave driver and wouldn't ease up. They danced as they talked about the competition. "We have to win first place! Nothing else will do!" He held his hand out and spun her around.

"You know, when we get older, we should turn professional and get paid to dance." She giggled.

"That would be cool. We could be another Fred and Ginger, like those movies Mhamo has us watch with her." Lucas chuckled.

"That would be so cool! I like Gene Kelly, myself. I enjoy watching him dance."

"Yeah, I just imagine I'm dancing with Melodi Carpenter." Lucas giggled. Melodi Carpenter was a girl from dance class that Lucas liked.

"She's too old for you, Lukie." Lilly chuckled.

"Doesn't matter; she's hot." He winked at Lilly. She giggled and shook her head.

"Lukie, I swear. What are we going to do with you?"

Lucas snorted and quoted a line from *Jailhouse Rock,* "Oh, Lils, it's just the beast in me."

"I didn't like that movie. He seemed like a jerk in it," Lilly admitted.

"I like the song. We should do a jive to it," Lucas suggested.

"That would be fun!" Lilly giggled. "We can dress like jailbirds."

"I don't look good in orange."

"Sparkly black and white stripes with fringe. I can make it for us."

"You do that, Lils; you do that." Lucas chuckled. "Thanks for being my partner all this time."

"You're welcome, Lukie. I'd do anything for you."

"And I would for you, too."

The kids were excited to go to the competition in Louisville. However, Lilly was bummed when they only placed second. She blamed herself, but it was Lucas who had missed a step. Still, they had a good time and brought home a ribbon and a small trophy.

Chapter Thirteen

Lucas had lived in Kentucky for five years now, and he was eager to go back and visit Jacob for his birthday. But, just before the trip, Deidre passed away and his trip was canceled. Jesse taught Lucas how to fight like a Marine, so when Matthew went on a bender Lucas put up his best fight. Jesse broke them up but not before he threw Matthew to the floor. "I told you, son! You'll never be able to fight me! Now straighten up!!" Matthew took a slug at him, but, instead, he found himself spinning and falling on the floor. "You're a disgrace to the Patrick name! Your mother would roll over in her grave if she saw how you treated her granddaughter. Beating on little kids!? After what your father put you through, you think you have the right to hurt them? Be a man, son!"

"You're not my father!"

"I'm more your father than Beau ever was!" Once again Matthew took a swing and missed. "Lucas, let's get out of here son. He's not going to hurt you anymore. You jackass!"

"He's my son!" Matthew got stern. "I'll discipline him how I like!"

"Over my dead body!" Jesse got firm.

"That can be arranged."

"Matthew you're not man enough to kill me. Now, go lay down on the couch and sleep it off." Jesse took the glass of whiskey Matthew tried to pour and threw it against the wall. "The last thing you need is a damn drink!" Matthew's eyes rolled in the back of his head, and he collapsed on the couch. "Good, he's passed out now. You alright?" Jesse asked Lucas.

Lucas wiped his mouth and shook his head yes. "Why didn't we just stay in New York? Did you know he was like this?"

"I knew he had a temper when he was drunk."

"And you let me live with him?" Lucas asked incredulously.

"Trust me, son, I regret it every day. We should have stayed in New York. We would have done something."

"We can always take Lilly and move back."

"Where would we live? Our home is here. You'll be eighteen in a few years, and you can go back then if you want."

"I'll take Lilly, and we'll return to Mama G's. We can all be a family again."

"I knew I should have never moved down here. We were worried about my health. Your Gigi isn't doing too good herself."

"What's wrong with her?"

"She's still upset over CJ."

"But Grandpa—"

"I know. I tried to get her to get help, but she refused. She won't talk about her at all. She's huddled up in her room, watching old Elvis movies, because she's depressed. I love you, Lucas, but more than that, I'm proud of you. You've been a great boy all your life. I know Matthew hurts, but I know in his way he loves you. You take the lessons he's teaching you each day and apply them to your life. Make something out of yourself. I know you can. We all know you can."

"What was Mom like? Will you tell me?"

"She—"

"Jesse!" Helen came around the corner, drunk and stern. "I told you don't talk about her!"

"Helen!" Jesse said exasperated. "Maybe—"

"She was MY DAUGHTER!"

"Helen we're not going to do this in front of the boy! He deserves to know about his mother!"

"She was MY DAUGHTER! I don't want to remember her like I saw her the last time in that casket! I see it when I close my eyes! I don't want to talk about her! I FORBID IT!"

"Let's go back to your room." He put his hand on hers, and Helen stood up tall. "If you need anything, Lucas ..."

"I know Grandpa."

Jesse escorted Helen back to their wing of Evergreen.

Chapter Fourteen

Despite everything Lilly had been through, she was a typical teenage girl in most ways. She wasn't big on pop culture but loved her teen idol, Jason Graham.

"Happy birthday, princess!" Lucas smiled at Lilly and handed her a card.

"To the best princess ever." She laughed because it was a card for a little girl even though she was turning sixteen. The more she read it, the harder she laughed. "JASON GRAHAM TICKETS!! ARE YOU SERIOUS?" She looked at him, stoked.

"I'm taking you to your first real concert. We're going to see him on the eighth."

"But, Lukie, that's your birthday. We always go bowling on your birthday."

"Lils, I can bowl anytime. You can't always see your future husband."

"You don't mind going with me?"

"Never!"

"So, I'm really going to see Jason Graham?"

"Look who's opening for him."

"Cindy Gibson! You get to see your wife, and I get to see my husband!" They giggled. "Come on, let's go to the Castle and plan our outfits." They held hands and ran up to their special spot, the rec room above Lilly's room, which they had dubbed *Crusader's Castle*.

When the big night came, Lucas was meticulous when getting ready. He shined his shoes, used too much hair gel, styled his hair perfectly, put on some aftershave, and brushed his teeth. He put on his white shirt and green suit with his pale pink blush tie.

I look good if I do say so myself.

"Ahhhhhhhh." He opened his mouth wide to stretch it out and smiled that million-dollar smile. "Who knows, Ashton, you might meet Miss Cindy tonight. There's always a chance she'll walk by the tour bus." He giggled, then went to get Lilly.

Lilly walked out of her bedroom in a poofy jean skirt with black leggings underneath, her hair teased to the ceiling, breaking the ozone layer with the amount of hairspray she'd used. She wore neon yellow earrings and a blue turtleneck underneath an oversized sweatshirt with *I Heart Jason Graham* on the front. She was a typical teenage girl. She had the biggest smile and was so excited. "I can't believe I'm going to my first real concert!"

"I know we've watched Echo a few times, but this—this is the big time." He grinned. Echo was Joe's band. They were still going strong picking up gigs all around the tri-state area.

She straightened up his tie. "You look snazzy."

"I feel snazzy. I bought this suit to wear tonight," Lucas admitted. "I know Cindy likes green. So, you never know." He giggled.

"If you meet her."

"You never know." Lucas chuckled.

When they made it inside Rupp Arena, Lilly made a beeline for the merchandise booth.

"I want a program!" Lilly said, buying a giant book filled with pictures of Jason Graham, her teen dream.

Lucas saw how much one was for Cindy. He also looked around and guessed at how much money a stand like this could take in, with girls buying the latest t-shirts and buttons. "Man, I bet they make a killing here."

"I bet. Look at this—$30 for a shirt."

"But it's got his picture on it." Lucas chuckled.

"I know; that's why I bought it."

"Be on the lookout, just in case she comes out here." Lucas laughed.

As Lucas looked at all the booths, he did some figuring in his head. He saw the opportunities for some big business. He was lost in thought when Lilly interrupted him.

"Want some?" Lilly had returned with a giant cone of cotton candy. She handed him his pop and some popcorn and pulled off some pink and blue confection for him.

"How much did you spend?"

"I spent way too much, but I'm having a good time."

"That's all that matters." He smiled at her as they headed to their seats in the nosebleeds.

"I hope we can see," Lilly said excitedly. "There's the stage!"

"They have giant monitors you can see, too." Lucas showed her.

"That's true. Oh, I'm so excited," Lilly squealed. "This is so different from Echo."

"Definitely different from Echo." Lucas giggled.

Before they knew it, the lights went down, and the music started blaring bubblegum pop. Lilly and Lucas held hands and squealed as the curtain went up. And there she was—Lucas's dream girl—in her spandex shorts, black shirt, and her little pork pie hat. Her straight blond hair hung down around her shoulders as the beat thumped through the arena. Girls all around danced around and waved their hands. Lucas and Lilly stood up, cheered, and screamed like everyone in attendance. They danced along to her biggest hits, *Only in Love* and *Staying Away*. They wrapped their arms around each other and sang at the top of their lungs.

"She's so hot!" Lucas chuckled as they watched her sit down and play the piano to the old Shirelles' song, "Will You Love Me Tomorrow?" Lilly and Lucas waved their hands as they sang along. Then she sang her song, *Dream Maker,* and threw her hat into the audience.

After Cindy did her set, a crew came out to prepare for the main event. Lilly was all smiles and happy as could be. Lucas was elated to experience this with her.

"You having fun, Lukie?" Lilly beamed brightly.

"I wanna do this," Lucas yelled over the loud music the arena played between sets.

"See if Joe can find a spot for you in Echo."

"No, I don't want to perform. I want to be behind the scenes. I want to make the big bucks."

"What do you mean?"

"I don't know what to do, but I know this is what I was born to do. I can get into the business side of the music business. I think I'd be good at it."

"You'll be great at it, Lukie! You can do anything you put your heart into. I have faith in you." Lilly smiled at him.

"Thanks, Lils."

They hugged as the lights went down again. Thunderous music blared from the stage. Lucas looked at Lilly, and she squealed like a little girl. She sat with her feet propped up against the bleacher in front of her. Her fingers folded against her mouth stomped her feet on the bleacher in excitement and bounced around. Lucas laughed heartily at his best friend and the magnetic hold Jason had on her. When the lights went down and Jason came out, Lilly shot up like a rocket, screaming like a banshee. She didn't care; she was excited. She jumped up and down and waved her hands in the air.

She's better than the show itself, Lucas thought.

When Jason came over to their side of the arena and waved to the crowd, Lilly yelled, "Lukie! He saw me! He waved and pointed directly at me!" she squealed in excitement. Lucas smiled at her but knew Jason couldn't see her. Lilly bounced around and giggled. She was living her teenage dream. Lilly took Lucas's hand and danced with him. They were so excited and happy to get to live this night tonight.

Lilly made friends with the girls around her as they swooned at how cute Jason was. Lucas had a few girls check him out, too. He smiled at them, and they giggled shyly. *Now this! I can get used to this!* Everyone went nuts watching Jason walk around in his tracksuit, singing songs everyone knew.

Two hours had passed, and the lights went down really low. Jason sat on the stage and serenaded a girl in the front row. When Jason waved to the crowd and said goodnight, Lilly's night was made, but she was heartbroken that it was over. Lucas saw her wiping her eyes. After the crowd yelled for a few minutes, Jason came back out for an encore, singing his biggest hit *Every Day Is Paradise (with You)*.

Lucas chuckled at the whole night, but he couldn't deny what Jason did to Lilly. She fell under his spell. Lucas watched Lilly and smiled as she swayed to the right and to the left, her arms in the air. When she wasn't singing, she squealed and bounced around to the rhythmic beat. When Jason said goodbye, he waved again toward where they were sitting.

"He waved to me, Lukie!" She giggled. Lucas smiled at her and let her believe in her dreams. They watched him leave the stage, and the lights came back on. Lilly sat there while everyone around her got their things and headed to the exit.

"What's wrong?" Lucas asked as he watched her calm down from her excitement.

"It's over." She looked at him pitifully. "My first concert is over."

"Did you have a good time?"

"I had the best time." She beamed brightly. "Thank you, Lucas. Thank you so much for getting the tickets and bringing me here. Thank you for spending your seventeenth birthday here with me. I'll never be able to repay you."

"Are you kidding? I had a blast! And I now know what I want to do with my life. This was an experience for me, too. This was the best time I've had in a long time."

"You mean it?"

"Of course! And, as always, it's with you." They hugged each other. Then, he took her hand and helped her down the stairs. As they were leaving, a younger girl told them she saw the tour buses.

Lilly got excited. "Are you going out to the bus?" Lilly asked the little girl.

"Yeah, I'm going to see if maybe they'll come out and sign autographs."

"Lukie!"

"Let's go!" They followed the girl and her mom down the stairs and out behind the arena.

Lucas looked around at a crowd of about fifty girls with their moms and friends. It was a cold January night, but everyone was so happy.

They sang, squealed, and danced around. Some even asked Lucas for his autograph because they thought he was with the group because of his suit. Other girls wanted to get a picture with him just because he was so cute. Lucas ate it up. Lilly laughed and took their pictures.

Lucas loved all the attention, but nothing—nothing—prepared him for what happened next. *Oh, my God! There she is!* Cindy Gibson came out, wearing an oversized green sweatshirt and a pair of jeans. She had a derby hat on and a smile on her face. She was only twenty feet from him. Then ten. Then five! Little girls squealed all around them, but Lucas couldn't hear anything except the sound of his heart beating in his chest. *She's signing Lilly's program!*

"It's my friend's birthday," Lilly explained. Lucas snapped back to reality. "Can you say 'Happy birthday, Lukie?'"

"Why sure." Cindy smiled at Lucas. "Happy birthday, Lukie!" Cindy chuckled and hugged Lucas. Lucas was stunned but thanked her. "I like your suit. Real snazzy."

"Thank you." Lucas grinned as she went on to the next group of girls. Lilly poked Lucas in the rib, and he couldn't hold back a squeal. Lilly laughed and hugged him.

"I hope that makes up for putting up with me all night?"

"Oh, my God." He chuckled. "I hope your boy comes out."

"Even if he doesn't, just the fact you got to meet her means the most to me." She smiled brightly and turned to a little girl. "Would you care to take our picture together?"

The girl's mom took the camera. They wrapped their arms around each other, held on tight, and smiled for the camera.

Chapter Fifteen

While everyone at school lived for spring break, Lilly lived for March Madness at Uncle John's house. It was a welcome break from her college courses for her astrophysics degree as well as her high school classes. John, Lucas, and Lilly gathered around the TV with their tournament brackets ready to watch tip-off.

"Okay, Squirrel and Jug, who do you have winning it all?"

"I want Big Blue, but, in all honesty, I think it's going to be Duke again."

"Yeah, I think you're right." John sighed and looked at his bracket.

"I have Syracuse," Lucas said.

"You're a dweeb." Lilly laughed. They sat around, watching TV, while snow fell heavily outside.

"I think we're going to have a blizzard this weekend," John announced.

"Good! We won't have to go back Sunday." Lilly laughed.

"Ugh, I HATE snow!" Lucas growled. "I hate the cold ever since Miss THANG here talked me into coming up last month and got us stuck."

"It's not my fault you didn't put gas in the car."

"It's not my fault you didn't put gas in the car," Lucas mocked her. "You're the one that was supposed to fill it up."

"You're the one that left his wallet at home with the spare change and LOCKED THE KEYS IN THE CAR! Yet it's MY FAULT for getting us stuck?"

John laughed as he watched them go back and forth.

"Well, you wanted to watch that stupid game," Lucas retorted.

"You wanted to see Kelly," Lilly reminded him.

"Kimberly,"

"Kimberly, Kylie, Kathy—whatever her name was—you wanted to see her." Lilly snickered.

"And I didn't get to, either. Instead, I. FROZE. TO. DEATH!"

"Well, I didn't get to watch my game, either."

"We're working out a system. You and Uncle John can call each other and talk on the phone while these games are on. I'm not freezing my butt off, coming up here just so you can watch a game." Lucas said.

"Oh, now, Jug, you had your excuses, too," John intervened. "Krissy—"

"Yeah, Krissy." Lucas laughed. "I knew it was a K name."

"—came over here to see you," John finished.

"She did? Where was I?"

"You went shopping with Sheryl, I think. You needed some hair gel and didn't trust her to get the right kind." He laughed. "Jug, you and your hair."

"It's styling and profiling." Lucas laughed heartily and fake-combed his bangs back with his hand.

"I know what it is! It's this!" Lilly got him in a headlock and gave him a noogie.

Lucas yelled and pushed her off. "Damn it, Liliana! I was having a good hair day!" He stormed off to the bathroom, while Lilly laughed herself silly.

"You're awful, squirrel."

"I know." Lilly laughed and sat back.

The next weekend while Lucas and Mary went to the movies, John and Lilly watched basketball.

"One more game, squirrel, and we'll be going to the Final Four!"

"Oh, Uncle John, I'm so excited!" Lilly giggled and bounced in her seat. "Do you think we can beat Duke?" Duke was the heavy favorite and national champion.

"I hope so!"

"I'm so nervous!" Lilly giggled.

"We got this, squirrel. If we can just overcome Laettner." Christian Laettner was a star player on Duke's team.

"I don't like him! He's cocky! Come on, boys!" Lilly cheered from her seat; John puffed on his cigar.

The game was close during the first half, with the teams exchanging leads back and forth. John and Lilly needed a nice break at halftime.

"Squirrel, I don't know if my heart can take this."

"I know, Uncle John. This is crazy! But they're doing so good."

They returned to their seats as Lucas and Mary came home and Sheryl came in from work.

"Okay, squirrel, twenty more minutes! Twenty more minutes 'til the Final Four."

Mary went into her room, while John, Sheryl, Lilly, and Lucas watched the end of the game. When a Kentucky player fell to the floor,

Christian Laettner, with his cocky smile, stomped on the player's chest. John and Lilly went ballistic!

"Now, that's bullshit!!" John scooted over the edge of his seat and pumped his fist at the TV.

The referees issued Laettner a technical foul but allowed him to continue playing. As play resumed, John and Lilly sat on the edge of their seats and cheered as if their life depended on this game. Duke pulled ahead, but then Kentucky tied the game with 33.6 seconds left on the clock. John and Lilly were ecstatic. Lilly jumped up and down and cheered like a fool.

"Are you actually crying?" Lucas laughed as he made fun of her.

"SHUT UP! We're almost to the Final Four! We're going into overtime. Oh, my God. We might win. We … we might get to go to the Final Four!!" Lilly was euphoric, and John shared the same excitement.

It was a stressful and exhilarating five minutes of overtime as the teams traded leads. Kentucky pulled ahead with a 98-96 lead, then much to Lilly and John's dismay, Laettner scored Duke's final six points, giving Duke a 102-101 lead.

Kentucky hit a shot over Laettner to put Kentucky ahead 103-102 with 2.1 seconds left. Lilly and Sheryl jumped from their seats in jubilation.

"We might beat Duke!" John scooted even farther over the edge of his seat in anticipation. "We might do it!" Then Lilly watched as the ball Laettner shot arced toward the goal and through the net. "NOO!!!" Lilly yelled and dropped to her knees. Game over 104-103, Duke. John and Lilly sat in shock, sadness, and rage. Lilly cried uncontrollably while John said some words he shouldn't have said. Sheryl tried to reason with them.

"Guys, it's just a game. They had a great season."

Lucas scolded Lilly for her over-the-top reaction. "Are you really crying that hard?" He chuckled. "It's just a game!"

"It's okay, squirrel. No one understands, but I do." Lilly sat on Uncle John's lap, wrapped her arms around him, and cried her heart out like she had so many times as a little girl.

"I have a new Patrick rule," John said. "From this day on, no Patrick now or ever will root for the Duke Blue Devils."

"John, now you're being silly," Sheryl said. "It's just a game!"

"They're trash, Uncle John. Trash! Absolute trash! I WILL ALWAYS HATE DUKE! I'll never root for them ever! Today, March 28th, will go down in history as the worst day ever!"

"Lilly, you're being overdramatic." Lucas laughed. "It's. Just. A. Game!"

"Son, if you say that one more time!" John scolded.

"Thirty years from now I'll still hear about this" Lucas laughed and watched as Lilly lay her head on Uncle John's shoulder. He held her as if her world collapsed in two.

Later that evening, Joe came home upset. "What's wrong, son?"

"Mark is a slime bag. He's been taking fifty percent. We caught him last night, so now I have to find a new manager," Joe said, frustrated.

"What does he do?" Lucas asked.

"Sets up gigs, makes sure we get paid, promotes us, things like that."

"I can do that. I can be your manager."

"Do you think you're up to it?" John asked.

"Yeah. Can you help me?" Lucas asked John.

John was in a popular rock band in the sixties, so he had experience. "Sure, son. I'll show you what to do."

"How much do I get paid?"

"The going rate is twenty percent. The more popular we get, the more everyone gets paid."

"Yeah, I think I can do that."

"You want to do it, man?" Joe asked.

"Yeah, I mean, I'm up here every weekend as it is. Why not?"

"Sure, I don't see why not," John said.

"Alright, little bro, I think this is going to be great." Joe and Lucas fist-bumped then embraced.

As he learned the ropes, Lucas realized he enjoyed the management business. He applied the lessons Matthew taught him. Under his management, Echo branched out of the tri-state area and went as far as Cincinnati. They had a local hit and recorded an album. Echo was in such high demand that at the end of the summer they loaded up their gear and headed west to California to try their luck at the big time. Lucas was undaunted, though. He lined up three more acts, and, with John's help, he formed Ashton Enterprises, a talent management agency. He was well on his way.

Chapter Sixteen

Mary and Lucas had always been friends, but as they got older, Lucas realized how much he liked her. She had long flowing brown hair and pretty green eyes. Lucas had several girlfriends both at home and in Ashland, but he really liked Mary. Her smile sent radiated through him. No other girl he dated matched what Mary's smile did to him. With John and Sheryl's blessing, they started dating. They were each other's first true love. Every weekend when Lucas came for a visit, he and Mary spent a lot of quality time together.

While Lucas and Mary dated, Lilly went out with the captain of the football team—and the hottest guy in school—Scott Irons. Lucas tried to be open-minded, but he didn't trust him. His "Lukie sense" kicked in. Scott was too perfect. He was too pretty (which really bothered Lucas), and he had all of the cheerleaders after him. He only noticed Lilly because she was friends with her basketball teammate and the resident hottest girl in school, Lexie Carmichael. *There's just something about him*, Lucas groaned to himself. *He better not hurt her!*

Lilly was crazy about the boy, but she wasn't ready for sex yet. Scott wanted to take things to the next level after the next school dance.

"Lukie, what am I going to do?"

"Do you want to?"

"I don't know. I'm scared to death! What if he hurts me? What if it hurts? I don't want to panic and embarrass myself. What if he tells the whole school or the whole football team? You know how I am about intimacy. I'm so scared."

"He won't say anything if he's a gentleman. Gentlemen treat ladies with respect. Does he respect you?"

"I ... uh ..." Lilly wasn't sure if he respected her. She was naive to intimate relationships. "I just ... I don't want to freak out." She looked at Lucas as she sat on her bean bag in Crusaders' Castle.

"I don't think you're ready then."

"What would you do if someone said that to you?"

"I'd understand and give her some time," Lucas said.

"I just ... I want it to be like it's supposed to be, like, you know, the romantic thing. I don't want him to think bad about me, and I'm afraid if I do anything, then he'll think bad of me."

"You've been going out for three months, right?"

"Yeah."

"Do you think you're ready?"

"I'm just so scared, to be honest."

"Then I don't think you're ready."

"I just ... I want to try it out before I do anything, you know? You know how I panic when people get close to me. You know how I don't like to be touched. I'm afraid someone will hurt me."

"You want to see how you'll react?"

"Yeah, I don't want to get there and freak out, you know. I don't want to embarrass myself. So, you think I should wait?"

"Yeah. If he starts pressuring you, then tell me and I'll take care of the problem for you. I'd do anything in the world for you, princess."

"I like him. I just ..." Lilly had a moment of bravery. "Maybe we could, ya know ... just do a practice run."

What the holy fuck? Lucas's eyes got big. "You want to with me?"

"Well yeah. I mean ... I won't freak out so bad if it's with you. I trust you."

"I—uh —I. Lils, I don't know," he said unsurely. *Oh, great Ashton! How are you going to get out of this one? You just said you'd do anything in the world for her!*

"It's okay if you don't want to. I just ... maybe I'll just break up with Scott. But I like him, and ... he's a nice guy, and he's cute, too." She giggled. There were a few moments of silence when Lilly's proposal hung in the air between them. "I don't want to break up with him. I really like him, Lukie. I just ... I'm so scared I'm going to embarrass myself. At least with you—"

"Lils"

"I mean ... how was it with you and Marie Compton?" Lucas's heart raced. The lie he told her and Joe when he was fourteen was coming back to bite him. At the time, he just wanted them to see him as cool, as a bad ass.

"Lils it's a lot. I don't think you're ready."

"But what if he breaks up with me?"

"Then he was no good."

"I know you don't like him."

"I know, but you do, so I put up with him. If he hurt you—"

"He won't hurt me. Will you, though?"

Lucas looked at her; his heart hammered in his chest. "I ... I ..." he saw her face. She looked pitiful, sad, and scared.

"What if I never can? What if I'm thirty years old and never have? Would anyone love me?" She asked sincerely.

Resigned that he wasn't going to get out of it, his mind raced. *I know it's weird. It's Lilly. She's like my sister. Hell, I call her my sissy, but what's the worst that can happen? It's one time, and no one will ever have to know. I can't let her down. But it's Lilly! Do you really ...*

Lucas opened his mouth to discourage her again, when the words he never meant to say came out. "Lils, if you really want to, we can."

What the fuck, Ashton! It's Lilly!

"I mean, I ..." she sighed, "I want to because I don't want to be scared for when it really does happen."

"You just have to have faith that you'll be okay."

"I'm so scared, Lukie."

"Then don't do it. Princess, if he's pressuring you, say no." *God, what am I going to do?*

"But I want him to like me."

"If he likes you, he'll be okay with waiting."

"Yeah, but what if he's not okay?" Lilly asked, scared.

"Then you need to dump him. He's bad news."

"I like him a lot."

"I don't know what to tell you, princess. I don't think you're ready. It's a big thing to go through."

"Yeah, I know," she said softly. She wiped the tears on her sleeve.

"Lilly, you'll be okay. I promise."

"You think so?"

"Yeah. I know you."

"So, do you think maybe Friday we can do a test run?"

"Are you really wanting to?" Lucas's heart raced. *She's not going to let this go, is she? What the hell have I gotten myself into? How can I get out of this? What about Mary?*

"If I do it with anyone, I want it to be you. At least you won't judge me."

"I'd never judge you, princess. What about Mary? What about Scott? What if they find out?"

"It will be our secret to keep forever! We won't tell anyone! No one!"

"Crusaders promise!" Lucas stuck his hand out.

"Crusaders promise!" Lilly took his hand, and they did their special handshake.

"How are we going to do this?"

"I say we get some of Matthew's bourbon and get drunk and then go for it." She laughed. "I mean no offense, but it's going to be weird. But at least I'll know if I can do it."

Thank God she agrees it's going to be weird.

"You can do it. I agree we get plastered, and then we do it, say, up in here?"

"Yeah, in our special spot."

"Okay." Lucas chuckled nervously.

"Are you okay with this? I don't want to pressure you."

"I'm okay with it. I am an old pro, you know," he said, lying through his teeth. He winked at her. *What am I supposed to say? 'No, Lilly, I lied?' I'm a world-class jackass! Oh, Ashton, you've done it this time.*

On Friday, Lilly sneaked several bottles of Matthew's booze up to their special spot in Crusaders Castle. By the time Lucas went up there, he was a nervous wreck.

How the hell do I get out of this? How can I do it and not hurt her? No, Ashton, be the best friend. What's the worst that can happen? It's just a one-time thing. Joe said it was great. He said just make sure to pull out. Remember that Ashton. My God, what am I getting myself into? How could I lie to her like that?

"I got some weed for us." Lucas laughed and pulled out a baggie.

They rolled a few joints and lit up.

"God, this shit is nasty," Lilly said, laughing as she puffed.

Lucas agreed but coughed and kept puffing away. "I feel calmer now, though."

Lilly opened a big bottle of Jack Daniels and took a drink, making a face. "God, this stuff tastes horrible." She laughed and handed the bottle over to Lucas.

I can't believe I'm doing this. He took a longer pull on the bottle. "Mary and I broke up."

"Really? Why?"

"Because I can't see her all the time. I'm only there on the weekends." He continued puffing away, enjoying the relaxing effect the weed had on his frazzled nerves.

"I'm sorry. I know how you liked her."

"I think I'm going to try to get back with her and take her to her homecoming next week."

"You should."

"Yeah, I ... I like her, Lils. I mean *really* like her."

"Then call her and talk to her and tell her you love her." She took a few more drags on her joint.

"I don't know," he sighed. "It's so hard, her being there and me being here."

"At least you get to see her on weekends."

"Yeah, that's true. Are you sure about this? I mean really, really sure?" *Please back away. I promise it won't hurt my feelings.*

"Yeah," she sighed, "I am. I want to get it over with, so I know what to expect tomorrow."

"Okay, Lils, I understand. I want you to make sure."

"Are you okay with doing this with me?"

Not in a million years. "Oh, yeah, I'll be fine." He chuckled nervously.

"Thank you, Lukie. I appreciate it."

"I love you, Lils. I'll do anything in the world for you."

"I'd do anything for you, too."

"Okay, let's do this."

Lucas giggled nervously, bumbling as he kissed Lilly. They chuckled, and drunkenly, clumsily, and shyly, they changed their lives forever. The second it was over they raced to put their clothes back on. For the very first time, there was a strange awkwardness between them. Sheepishly, Lucas was the first to speak.

"Are you okay? Did I hurt you?"

"No, I'm okay. That wasn't as bad as I thought it was going to be," she admitted.

"Um, thanks? I think?"

"No, I mean ..." Lilly blushed, "I made it through that. I didn't freak out. I think I'll be okay."

"I hope so, Lils. I think you'll be okay."

"Thanks, Lukie." "You're welcome, princess." They looked at each other, not sure what to say or where to go forward. They were both innocent best friends—she was his princess and he was her Lukie—and now they had crossed a line they never imagined they'd cross. But it was a one-time thing, and no one would ever find out.

Lilly ran her hands up and down her arms and looked at Lucas again. *Did I hurt him? He was so brave to do this for me. He's such a good friend.* Her thoughts were interrupted when *Ain't No Mountain High Enough* played on the radio. That was always their song. There was nothing they wouldn't do for each other. Nothing could stop them from getting to the other, but, as she watched Lucas stare out the window, Lilly wondered if maybe he'd done too much for her. Had she asked too much?

Lucas stared at the night sky. His mind was in a daze. Lilly was his best friend. He'd loved her since they were little, but never romantically. She was always just there, and now he had had sex with her. He wasn't sure how he felt. *I feel awkward. I'm not in love with her, but I feel weird doing that with my best friend. I imagined my first time might be with Mary next week. We talked about it a few times, but ... do I tell her? I mean, Lilly is just Lilly. We aren't in love with each other. She was just scared. Did I do the right thing? Normally I would talk to Lilly about it but I can't. You're going to be ok Ashton. Things will be fine. Tomorrow is a new day. You'll go to the dance and she'll be ok. Things are going to be alright.*

Chapter Seventeen

Lucas, his date Elyse, Lilly, and Scott attended the school dance together. Things were going okay until Lucas caught Scott checking out other girls. When he saw Scott hit on Isla Carmine, he lost it. "Stay away from her!" Lucas got in Scott's face.

"Relax ... *Lukie*," Scott snickered. Lucas drew back to punch him, but Lilly came back at that moment. She looked at Scott like he hung the moon. She hadn't seen them arguing but knew something was wrong. "Lilly! He's hitting on other girls! Look at him. He's asking Isla to dance."

"It's just one dance. I dance with you all the time."

"Lilly he's been hitting on other girls. I saw him kissing Jenny Hawthorne."

"She's his best friend."

"Liliana!"

"He's not a bad guy!"

"Lilly he's bad news!" Lilly cuddled up to Scott. Scott snarled at Lucas, wrapped his arm around Lilly,

"See you around, Luckie." Scott snickered and walked away with Lilly on his arm. Lucas saw Elyse hanging out with her friends. They were looking at Scott. Lucas rolled his eyes, growled and went to Jeremy Roach's secret stash of beer. He needed a break.

After homecoming, Scott tried to get Lilly to go to the hotel with him, but she couldn't. Her heart raced as she watched his reaction to her rejection.

"I'm sorry, Scotty, I can't. I'm not ready."

"Not ready? It's been three months! When will you ever be ready?" He raised his voice to her, and Lilly panicked, her eyes wide with fear.

"You know what? I don't need this. Find me when you're 'ready.' I'll see you around."

"You son of a bitch!!" Lucas, who was standing nearby with Elyse, overheard their conversation. He punched Scott square in his pretty face then returned to mend Lilly's broken heart.

"You were right, Lukie! He wasn't a good guy after all! I'm so stupid!" Lilly sobbed in her hands. Lucas wrapped his arm around her and held her as she cried.

"I got you, princess. He's an asshole. He didn't deserve you. One day, someone will come into your life and make Scott Irons a bad memory. I know it hurts now, but there will come a day when you'll look back at this whole weekend and laugh."

"I just couldn't, Lukie. I can't—someone seeing me like that."

"I know, Lils."

"Will I ever be normal?"

"Yeah, you're going to be fine. Someday you'll find the right guy and fall in love. You might even leave me behind." Lucas laughed.

"I'll never leave you, Lukie. I don't care who it is. If he can't handle us, then I don't need him. Crusaders never abandon each other. You're a Crusader; you come first."

"You mean that?"

"Of course, I mean that! I'd walk through fire for you, Lucas Ashton. There's nothing I wouldn't do for you."

"Nothing I wouldn't do for you either, princess."

"Crusaders Pledge!" Lilly announced.

"I promise to protect you with all my heart at all times," they said in unison.

"I love you, Lils."

"I love you, too, Lukie." He hugged her tightly.

A few weeks after the dance, Lilly felt flushed, tired, and nauseous. She couldn't keep anything down. "I feel horrible," she whined to the school nurse.

"Could you be pregnant, Miss Patrick?" the nurse asked after a brief exam.

She knew about sex came from rock videos and things other kids saidn the videos and heard him on the radio and"Uh, I ... I ... I don't know. You can't get pregnant on your first time when you're a virgin! I mean—" Lilly let it hang in the air, embarrassed that she had to tell a nurse that. The nurse looked over her glasses at Lilly. "Miss Patrick, you can get pregnant by having sex the first time. It happens quite often."

"It does? But ... I ..." Lilly looked around to see if anyone was watching. "It ... it was once, and he said he pulled out. Joe said you can't get pregnant if you ... ya know." Lilly was embarrassed she had to explain to an adult how things worked.

"Miss Patrick, the only foolproof method is abstinence. How long have you been feeling like this?"

"A few days." Lilly's heart raced a mile a minute. "I can't be. What do I do?"

"I suggest you get a test."

"I just ... I can't be! It's ..."

"I suggest speaking with the baby's father, as well."

Oh my God, I can't be! Lilly looked at the nurse with terror in her eyes.

"Good luck, Miss Patrick." The nurse was sending Lilly back to class.

Instead, she paced the hallways until the release bell rang, trying to make sense of it all. *No way can I be pregnant! It was just one time. What would I do with a baby? No, it's just silly. I have the flu. There's just no way! It's just crazy!* She went to Albertson's Drug Emporium, not even completely sure what to look for. She was too embarrassed and ashamed to ask a pharmacist. She didn't want the old man to look over his glasses at her and judge her the way he judged the old lady in front of her who was getting her prescription as Lilly walked in.

Which one do I get? She wanted to be invisible.

"Can I help you miss?" The pharmacist with the glasses had appeared out of thin air, doing the one thing she didn't want him to do—talk to her.

Lilly's face turned red. She didn't know what to do or ask, so she picked up a bottle on the shelf. "Found it!" She forced a smile.

He gave her a perplexed look and walked away. Lilly's heart thumped in her chest as she the enema back and then picked the most expensive test she could find. *It's expensive, so it must be good.* She nonchalantly picked up several items she didn't need so it wouldn't be obvious what she was buying. She found a logic puzzle magazine she was happy to see and, in a shameful, scared, and embarrassed way, checked out.

Lilly drove home and tried to put the test out of her mind. *What am I going to do with a baby? I can't have a baby. Where would I keep it? I mean ...*

Lilly went to her room. She sat the bag on her dresser, pulled out the logic puzzle, and took it to her desk, trying to focus on something other than that test. But the bag tormented her from across the room. "I'll do it later," she said to herself. "There's no sense in being scared. I'm not pregnant."

"Pregnant?" Lucas asked as he came into her room. Lilly looked at him. Her heart thumped in her chest.

"I ... I ..."

"What?!" Lucas looked at her with wide, scared eyes.

"I haven't felt well and ..."

"And what, Liliana?!" he demanded.

"The nurse at school thought I might be pregnant."

"That's crazy!"

"I know. That's why I said I'd take the test later. I wasted money on it. There's no way I can be pregnant. Who would think it?" Lilly chuckled.

"But you haven't felt good for a while."

"I know," Lilly sighed.

"Lilly, maybe you should ..."

Lilly looked at the bag for the thousandth time. She didn't want to face the chance she might be. "I just can't be," she said softly.

"You better check." Lucas handed the test to her.

"How do I ..."

"Read the instructions."

"Will you ..."

"I'll be right here with you." Lilly shakily took the package.

"Lukie, I'm scared," she admitted as the fear of not knowing caught up with her.

"We'll get through this together."

"Crusader's pledge."

"I promise to protect you with all my heart at all times," they said in unison.

"You can do this, princess."

Lilly squeezed his hand and stepped into the bathroom.

Lucas glared at the white door as it shut. *She can't be pregnant. It was only one time. We were virgins. Virgins can't get pregnant. I pulled out! Joe said you can't get pregnant if you pull out. What will I do if I'm a dad? How will we ... Oh, Mama. Help me, please.*

Lilly opened the door and came out with the test. "Says we have to wait a few minutes. What are we going to do if—"

"It's not going to come back positive. It can't be positive. We're too young to be parents. We're not even dating," Lucas tried to rationalize.

After the longest few minutes in their young lives, Lilly and Lucas held hands as they looked at the test together.

"It says—"

"Positive," Lilly said shakily and dropped the test. "I ... I ... I can't ... we ... we ... we ..." Lilly looked at Lucas as his eyes shut and he fell to the floor. "Lukie! Lukie!"

He opened his eyes to Lilly gently tapping his cheek.

"Huh?" He looked around, shaken up. "What happened?"

"You passed out. Are you okay?"

"Uh," he tried to speak, but words wouldn't come out. "Pregnant?"

"Yeah," Lilly cried. "I don't know what to do! What do I do now?"

"I ... I ... we can give it up for adoption," Lucas offered. "Or we can ..."

"What?" Lilly asked innocently.

"Rebecca Gershmire went to a clinic."

"What kind of clinic?"

"A clinic where they make you not pregnant anymore."

"What do they do?"

"Look up abortions. That's what she had," Lucas said.

"What do they do when they do that?"

"I don't know. Lilly, what are we going to do?"

"I don't know we'll … we'll figure something out."

"Maybe Gigi can help us. She'll know what to do."

"I don't know what to do, Lukie! I'm scared. I'm so scared." She flopped on her bed and cried her heart out.

"I'm so sorry." Lucas sat next to her and put his head in his hands. "Maybe we should go to the library and see what happens at that clinic."

"If I go, will you go with me?"

"Of course! I'll never let you face anything like that alone. We'll get through all of this together! Crusaders pledge!" They held hands and said their pledge.

Chapter Eighteen

Lilly and Lucas decided to talk to a nurse at the clinic before making a decision. As they sat down, Lilly grabbed Lucas's hand. "Everyone is judging me," Lilly told him.

"No one is judging you."

"The old lady across from us is looking at me disgusted."

"Just ignore her."

"I don't know if I can do this, Lukie."

"We don't have to do anything today. We need to find out what happens, and then we can go from there."

"I don't want to hurt anyone. I don't want people to think bad of me."

"Don't worry about what people think."

The nurse called for them, and Lilly held onto Lucas's hand as they walked to the exam room.

"How may I help you?" The nurse looked at them kindly.

"We want to know what happens," Lucas said.

"Let's run some tests and then we'll explain." Lilly changed into a gown and had an ultrasound. "That's your baby." Lilly squeezed Lucas's hand as the nurse explained what happened during the procedure. "It is an option you have if you choose to. Do your parents know?"

Lilly gasped. In all of this, she hadn't even considered telling Matthew. *What is he going to do to me? He'll kill me for real.*

"You'll need parental permission to perform it since you're underage. Do you have a doctor?"

"No, I don't have anything. We ... it ... it was one time and ... we're ..."

"It's okay. I understand. I see it all the time." The nurse opened the drawer and pulled out some pamphlets. "Look these over and talk with your parents. I suggest you weigh the pros and cons and determine what's best for you. You always have the option for adoption. Just know that, whatever you decide, we're here for you. You won't have to go through this alone, and we're completely safe."

"Thank you," Lilly said. The nurse walked out. "Lukie, I can't do that I can't go through that. The procedure ... the baby I ... that's ... that was our baby. I can't harm the baby."

"I know, princess. We can raise it. Unless you want to give it up for adoption?"

Lilly's head spun with confusion. "I don't know what to do."

"How about we talk to Gigi and Grandpa and see what they say? One way or the other, we'll do what's right."

When they returned from the clinic, Lucas and Lilly talked to Jesse and Helen.

"Kids," he said, devastated. "What are you going to do?"

"We don't know," Lilly said.

"It was a one-time thing—" Lucas started.

"It's my fault. I'm sorry," Lilly said somberly.

"It's okay, Lillybug."

"What's done is done. We'll get through this together. Have you told your father?" Helen asked.

"No. I was afraid to."

"He's not going to take the news well."

"I know. Can you be there when we tell him? He listens to you better," Lilly asked Jesse.

"I'll be there for you every step of the way." Despite the way he felt, Jesse smiled at Lilly. He had to be there for her.

That evening Jesse got everyone together after dinner. "Son, we need to talk. The kids have some news."

Lilly's heart felt like it was going to explode.

"What is it, Liliana?" Matthew asked.

"I-I …" she stammered. She squeezed Lucas's hand and looked to Jesse for reassurance. He nodded, and she moved her seat closer to him and took his hand. "It … I was … you're … you're going to kill me."

"It's killing me, this anticipation. I have had a long day. What is it?" Matthew asked as he took a drink of his bourbon.

"I'm …"

"She's pregnant," Helen blurted out, tired of the build-up.

"HELEN!" Jesse scolded.

Matthew sat there, considering the news. He was eerily quiet.

"Son," Jesse consoled, "As I told the kids, we can get through this together. No need to do anything crazy."

Matthew swirled his drink in quiet contemplation while everyone stared at him, trying to gauge his reaction. "If you will excuse me," he said, finally moving his seat out from the head of the table and walking away.

"What's he doing?" Lucas asked. They heard his heavy footsteps marching down the hallway.

"Brace yourself, kids. Who knows what he's going to do, now that he knows." Jesse said.

Lilly squeezed Lucas's hand.

"MR. ASHTON!!!!" Matthew screamed venomously and sarcastically as he stormed back into the dining room with a shotgun pointed right at Lucas. "You stupid son of a bitch! You got that whore pregnant! You're going to pay now!"

"MATTHEW!!!" Jesse shouted. "Put that gun down!!! Put it down right now!!!"

But Matthew didn't listen. Helen freaked. "Matthew, please!"

"He knocked her up!! Your grandson knocked that slut up! He's going to pay!"

Lilly stepped in front of the gun. Her heart thumped in her chest, and her breathing was tight.

"LILLY, NO!!!" Lucas said behind her.

"Crusaders Pledge, Lukie! I'm enacting it. It's okay, Lucas, my life is over. Yours doesn't have to be," she said over her shoulder before facing Matthew and challenging him. "SHOOT ME!!! Go ahead and shoot me!! End my life. End this baby's life!"

"LILIANA!!!" Jesse and Lucas yelled.

"It's okay, Grandpa. I'm not afraid to die. I can't let Lukie pay for my mistake!"

Matthew cocked the gun. "Are you sure about that?"

"Yes, I'm sure!" Lilly shook, tears pouring down her cheeks. "I'd do anything for Lucas. Please, I beg you, don't hurt him, Daddy."

"Son, do you really want to go to jail for murder? For murdering your daughter and grandchild? Do you want the Patrick legacy that your mom worked so hard for to be remembered for this? Come on, son, put the gun down.," Jesse reasoned with him. "Come on, son. Do what's right. You don't want to hurt either of them. You love them. Lucas is the son you never had. Lilly is your daughter. Put the gun down, son. Don't do this. Be a man. Put it down."

Once the anger subsided, Matthew lowered the gun.

"Now hand it to me" Jesse reached his hand out, and Matthew pushed his hand away and raised the gun back.

"MATTHEW!!!" Jesse said in his stern Marine voice. "Put the gun down now!"

"GET OUT OF THE WAY, DAD!" Jesse stepped in front of Lilly.

"NO!!! You can kill me, but you're not going to kill these kids!!"

"Grandpa!" Lucas shrieked and reached out Jesse's arm.

"JESSE!!!" Helen yelled in fear.

"I'm not going to let your mother's legacy go down in flames because her son is an idiot! NOW. PUT. THE. GUN. DOWN!!!" He stood toe to toe with Matthew, as Matthew continued to glare at Lucas. Jesse saw his opportunity and charged after him, pushing the gun to point at the ceiling. Lucas knocked Lilly to the ground and covered her with his body. Helen screamed. Jesse wrangled for the gun as a shot went off and plaster exploded and dropped on their heads.

"YOU SON OF A BITCH!!!" Jesse snatched the gun away. "You could have killed someone!!!" He watched as Matthew—still stewing—realized what he had done, turned on his heel, and walked off. While Helen called 911, Jesse checked on the kids. "That was the last straw! We're all going to move to the lake house. He never goes down there. He could have killed someone!" Jesse said.

"Police are on their way." Helen noticed Jesse grabbing his chest. "Are you okay?"

"Yeah, just a little too much excitement," he chuckled grimly. "We're going to get through this together. You kids get your stuff packed. We'll move in while he's in jail. We can all take care of each other. I don't know what's wrong with him, but a few nights in jail might do him good."

Lilly sat on her bed and cried into her hands. *If I wasn't such stupid trash, none of this would have happened! My life is over, but I am going to love this baby and give it a name. I'll give it a life full of love and happiness. I'll give it everything I never had. I'll raise you on my own. Just the two of us, baby. It will be just the two of us. Lucas can go back to New York. He has his whole life ahead of him. He doesn't need me; he has enough on his plate. You'll hear about how great your dad was. He might even see you, but I'm going to set him free. He doesn't need to be tied down to us. It's my fault. I'll take care of us.*

At the same time, Lucas sat on the bed in his room. *What am I going to do now? How are we going to raise a baby? We were going to go back to New York. What would Mama G think if she knew? I can handle a lot, but I can't handle her being disappointed in me. God, I knew I should have said something! I should have said no. Ashton, you've done it this time, son.*

A few days later, Matthew was released from jail after talking with the judge and paying a hefty fine. Lilly rolled her eyes, knowing nothing was going to happen. Jesse told John about what happened and the pregnancy. John heard about the gunshot and called Lilly.

"Liliana, I'm so disappointed. You were always such a good girl."

"Uncle John," Lilly cried. John was quiet for a few moments; then he cleared his throat. The next words to come out of his mouth broke her heart. "Liliana, I love you, but I think you both should stay there from now on."

"What? Why?" she asked, hurt.

"You know how Mary felt about Lucas," John spoke firmly and fatherly.

"I know. He doesn't love me. He loves her. They got back together and have been together for a long time. He doesn't love me at all. It was a one time thing, a mistake."

"Yeah, well, choices were made. I think it's best for everyone if you two stay away. I don't want to hurt Mary anymore."

"I knew it was too good to be true that you would love us unconditionally," she said sadly.

"Liliana," he said, emotionless.

"No, Uncle John, it's okay. I love you. Have a good life." She hung up and cried her heart out. *I've ruined everything!!!! He's right! I'm nothing but stupid trash! I've always been stupid trash. Only trash gets pregnant this young.*

Chapter Nineteen

Jesse, Helen, Lucas and Lilly have been living in the lake house since the altercation. Matthew used his charm and apologized to everyone after he spent a few nights in jail. Lilly forgave him, but the rest were skeptical. He asked that everyone meet at the main house for Christmas dinner. While Lucas was skepitcal, Lilly extended an olive branch and accepted. Despite everything he was her father. It was a pleasant Christmas with the exception of Helen being sick.

It was a tense holiday season, but it was now Lucas's eighteenth birthday. "Happy birthday, Lukie!" Lilly smiled and served him his favorite dinner—homemade baked ziti and ravioli. It was a birthday tradition she'd done for years.

Jesse said, "You're eighteen, son! I am so proud of the fine young man you grew up to be. Your mom—"

"Jesse!" Helen gave him a stern look. Jesse sighed.

"Anyway, I just wanted you to know I'm proud of you," Jesse took Helen's hand, "but we have to talk."

Lucas's heart sank, and he took Lilly's hand and squeezed it. "This feels like it did when you said we were moving down here."

"I ..." Helen started. "You ..."

"What is it, Gigi?" Lucas asked.

Helen put her hand to her mouth and turned into Jesse's arm. He wrapped his arm around her. "I had a doctor's appointment today. I got some news that's hard to hear. I have terminal lung cancer. I have six months to live."

"NO!!!" Lucas yelled. "They can do things. There are—"

Helen shook her head.

"NO! We have to fight it! We'll get the best doctors. I'll do anything to help," Lucas said.

"Yeah, me, too," Lilly said.

"I just need to make these next few months the best ever. I need you to be patient with me. I'm going to be going through a lot. I do love you, Lucas. I hope I'm around to see your baby. I get to be a great Gigi." Helen hugged Lucas.

Lilly noticed Jesse was looking pale.

"You okay, Grandpa?"

"I'm okay, Lilly bug. It's just been a stressful few weeks. We'll get through this together, all of us. We're a family, and we take care of each other. I'm excited to be a grandpa again. I get to be a great grandpa."

"You're the best grandpa already" Lilly smiled and hugged Jesse. "I don't know what I would have done all these years if you hadn't stuck up for us."

"I can't believe how abusive he got. I remember his mom saying Beau was abusive, but I never dreamed he'd start it up on you. I wish I had known before we moved down here. We wouldn't have moved down here. We would have done something else. We would have tried to get custody of you."

"It's all right. I was used to it. He's shoved a gun in my face before."

"Is that why Melinda did what she did?" Jesse asked.

"I don't know. She could have taken me, but she left me. No one has ever wanted me." Lilly said somberly.

"Hey, bug! I want you!" Jesse said.

"Me, too!" Lucas said. Helen nodded.

"Thank you," Lilly smiled. She put her hand on her belly. "I can feel the baby moving." She took Lucas's hand and put it on her belly. He smiled at the feeling.

"I remember feeling Lucas move inside CJ," Jesse said.

"Will you tell me what she was like?" Lucas asked Gigi.

"Someday I'll write a letter when I can talk about it. Then you'll know all about her. It just hurts too hard to talk about her, even after all of these years. You'll understand when the baby is born. I hope you have a healthy baby."

"Thank you, Gigi."

It was now March. Life had been stressful the past couple of months, with Helen's chemo making her exhausted and Lilly's hormones turning her moody and emotional. Lilly had been in a downward spiral. She let herself go. She didn't shower. She hardly ate. She slept all the time and cried when she wasn't asleep. Lucas worried about her. It was more than teenage hormones or pregnancy. Lucas found her a few times playing with a knife. He distracted her while he pulled the knife away. He found empty pill bottles she claimed to have spilled. Lucas knew better. He finally got her in to see a doctor, who stared her on a regimen of healthier foods, moderate exercise, and journaling.

When she started doing better, he was relieved. "I can face anything with my Crusader by my side," he told her one evening when they were both in good spirits.

JUST THE TWO OF US

"I'll always be by your side, Lukie," she answered.

Now those words rang in Lucas's ears as he searched the house for her after not seeing her all evening. Finally, he saw a curtain billowing in the wind on the back terrace. He went to close the door and found her standing there. His heart raced in his chest as she spoke to him without turning around, her voice sounding cold and disconnected from reality.

"It's not that far of a fall. I'm sure no one would care. It'd be a big relief to them. I could set you free, Lucas. You wouldn't ever have to be tied down to me again. Crusaders pledge to look out for each other. I'm looking out for you."

"Crusaders pledge, Liliana," Lucas said firmly. "Remember Crusaders rule number one? Crusaders never abandon each other!"

"But you'd be free of me. You could pack up tomorrow and go back to New York and never have to worry about coming back here again," she pleaded her case with giant tears running down her cheeks.

"I might be free, but I'd lose my heart," Lucas said tenderly. "What's the point in living if I have to do it without you? You stepped in front of a loaded gun for me, not knowing if that might be the last breath you take."

"You—" she started with a quiver in her voice.

"How many times, Liliana, have you come to my defense and got yourself hurt to stop me from getting beat?"

"You—"

"No. How many times have you saved my ass from kids at school when I was the new kid? How many times have you gone *mama tiger* on people who made fun of me?"

"Lukie." Tears streamed down her face.

"I'm returning the favor, Liliana. I'm not letting you do this. We'll get through this. We'll power through everything like we always do because we're the Double L Crusaders. We fight for each other and are there for each other through thick and thin, richer and poorer, sickness and in health."

"Are we getting married?" she asked.

"Point is," he chuckled, "we are a team. We're a pair. We're bonded. You're hurting right now, and, no, it's not fair what's happening, but we can overcome it. We're two tough cookies; you know that. So, come on." He reached out his hand. Lilly could see his face was covered in tears. "Come closer and step away from the edge."

With the wind blowing through their hair, Lilly took Lucas's hand and let him pull her back onto the terrace. They cried on each other's shoulders.

"Don't ever do that to me again," he scolded her. "I can take a lot of things, but I can't take living without my best friend." He held her close.

"I'm sorry," Lilly whimpered. "I thought it would just be an easy fix to everyone's problems."

"It just makes my heart hurt worse. Now come on."

Lucas led Lilly back into the house with his arm around her and her head on his shoulder. "I thought you were taking your medicine?"

"It makes me think things. Lukie, I'm scared." Lilly held on to him.

"I know, princess. I am, too, but you got this. Besides, it's your holiday! We'll watch basketball and celebrate. I even made some green beer for you." Lucas laughed.

"I can't drink beer! I'm pregnant!"

"You big boob! This is nonalcoholic beer."

"They're sore, is what they are," Lilly whined.

"Come on." He put a St. Patrick's Day hat on her and a lei of clovers. "O Danny boy, the pipes, the pipes are calling," Lucas sang to her. "That's what I wanted. I wanted to see that smile. Come on, I have some corned beef and cabbage ready for you." Lucas poured her a stein of green frothy beer. "Top o the morning to ya, Miss Patrick," Lucas said in a horrible Irish accent.

"Mhamo would shit if she heard you."

"I miss her."

"Me too. She'd be a great-great Mhamo!"

"I think about her a lot."

"You were her Bulbie" Lilly chuckled at Deidre's nickname for Lucas.

"Bulbie," Lucas giggled.

Lucas and Lilly went into the living room with their green beer and Irish food. "To Ireland!" Lilly toasted. "Without you, I wouldn't be here." Everyone chuckled.

"To the Patricks! For always being my family!" Lucas raised his stein.

"Here, here! I've been blessed to know so many Patricks, and every one of them has been great. Especially my favorite Patrick, Patrick Ewing." Jesse laughed.

"Grandpa!" Lilly giggled.

"He won me $1,000 on a bet once! John was so mad. I think that's the last time he ever bet anyone."

"I wish he wasn't so upset with me."

"He'll be okay, Lillybug. He's got things going on he doesn't want to talk about. He won't even tell me."

"But you're his dad."

"I know, but you'll understand when your baby comes. Sometimes you have to just let them make their own choices. It's hard, but you have to let them go."

"Did you ever meet his real dad?" Lucas asked.

"No, I came after he passed. His mom told me about him. He was an evil bastard. He all the time tried to pit her against the kids. He was abusive to Matthew. She divorced him a few times, but they always got back together. That's how John came along. They remarried, and nine months later, here came John. Maisi, that's what I used to call her, said he never abused John, but he was all the time abusing Matthew. He was an evil drunk. He hit Maisi once, and she got a shotgun after him," Jesse laughed. "If you knew your grandma, you'd be proud of her. She was sharp as a tack. Nothing got past her. She knew the business inside and out. If she didn't like something, she changed it. She didn't care what anyone else thought. She was just like Deidre. They were both trailblazers. Deidre made Mary sign a prenup to protect the family name. She kept the name Patrick. Just think; you could have been Liliana Holston."

"Really?"

"Mary refused to have the boys take his name. They were to be Patricks. They were her legacy."

"Did you sign a prenup?" Lucas asked.

"I did. I would get a fair settlement if we divorced, but that never happened. We loved each other and were together until her dying day. It's been so long, but I still miss her. However, I wouldn't give up my life now for anything. I have my family right here." Jesse held his arms out for Lucas, Lilly, and Helen. "And I love all of you with whatever's left of my wounded ticker." Jesse gave a jovial laugh.

"We love you, too, Grandpa." Lilly kissed his cheek. Thank you for helping us and for saving us so many times."

"Lilly bug, there's nothing I wouldn't do for you." He kissed her cheek and laid his head against her head. Helen had dozed off in her chair, so Jesse gently woke her and helped her up to go to their room. "Come on, Mom. You're getting tired. Let's get you to bed."

As Lucas watched them walk slowly toward their room, a sudden sadness came over him that he couldn't shake. *Mama, please watch over all of us.* Then he turned to Lilly and hugged her.

"You okay?" Lilly asked.

"Yeah, I just ... I want to be able to tell the baby about my mom, and I'll never get the chance to."

"Maybe you can get Grandpa alone and ask him."

"Maybe I will. I'll see if he wants to take a ride tomorrow and ask him. I'm glad you know about your grandmother, Miss Holston." Lucas chuckled.

"I'm glad she put a stop to it. I like the Patrick name. Well, Lukie, let's get this place cleaned up. Thanks for my St. Me Day party."

"St. Me," Lucas chuckled. "You're welcome Lils. You're welcome."

Chapter Twenty

Lucas held Helen's hand as she sat heartbroken and stunned. When she and Jesse had gone to bed on St. Patrick's Day, Jesse's heart gave out.

"I can't believe it." She paused choked back tears. "Lucas, what am I going to do now? He was my life. We were married for thirty years. My heart has been ripped out of my chest. I don't know how I can go on."

As Helen sobbed, Lucas wrapped his arm around her.

"How am I going to get through tomorrow? The next day. He was my rock. He was my everything. He looked so handsome in his University of Kentucky sweatshirt and jeans. That's how I met him. He came up to New York with Matthew. I was stranded with CJ on the side of the road in the middle of nowhere. A blizzard hit, and it was so cold. Jesse saw us and asked me in that deep Southern drawl of his if he could help us. I didn't have a spare tire, and CJ was cold and hungry. He asked me if he could take me home and come back tomorrow with a tire. Something in his eyes told me to say yes. He took us home, and then his car got stuck. All the tow trucks were out. He said at least he got me home. I couldn't let him and Matthew walk to a hotel anywhere. He said he didn't mind the walk, that he was a Marine and had seen a lot worse. Right away, I felt safe with him. I insisted he stay. I made dinner and put CJ to bed, and the three of us stayed up all night, talking and getting to know one another. We bonded over hot cocoa and vegetable soup. We played cards and listened to the radio. The next morning, we were able to get his car out. He saw how bad my tires were and insisted he buy me four new snow tires. He said, 'I can't let a pretty girl like you get stranded, Miss Cast.' He always called me Miss Cast. After he bought the tires for me, I drove home heartbroken that I'd never see him again. He said he had to go back to Kentucky, but he hoped to see me again.

"A week passed, and I couldn't get him out of my mind. Then, I opened the door one day, and he was standing there in his Marine's dress blues. God, Lucas, he looked so handsome. He had a bouquet of daisies because he knew I liked them, and he asked me if I'd go out on a date with him. I said I'd love to, but I had to let him know CJ came first. He said he'd raised two rambunctious boys, and he'd like to try raising a girl. 'How hard can they be?' he asked." She touched Lucas on the arm with surety.

"That's when I knew, Lucas. I just knew. We went to the movies and then for a ride in Central Park. The next day, he went to a daddy-daughter lunch with CJ. After a week, I knew I was in love. He said he had to go back to Kentucky, but he'd come up here one more time. My heart ached when he left. He came back in his uniform again, with more flowers. Well, we went for a ride, and he took me to this house he'd found. It was a cute little house. It was done up just right. I told him I loved the house but couldn't afford it. He said, 'Miss Cast, it only costs $35.' I asked him why it was $35. He said, 'That's how much a marriage certificate for the state of New York costs.' That was his marriage proposal! On the porch of that house, he got down on one knee and asked me to marry him. He said, 'I promise never to break your heart, and a Marine always keeps his promises.'" Helen sobbed into her tissues. "That's the only lie he ever told me because he died on me, breaking my heart. Oh, Lucas." Helen put her head in her hands and cried her heart out as Lucas held her close to him.

It was now the end of June, everyone was on baby watch. Jessica Lauren Patrick Ashton, after her grandfather, was due to arrive any day. Lucas sat in the living room with Helen. Even though she had gotten weaker, she still enjoyed watching old Elvis movies. Lucas had seen *Clambake* more times than he could count, yet he'd sit through it every time because it made Helen happy. Elvis was singing the silly song "Do the Clam" when he heard Lilly scream.

"LUCAS!!" Lilly yelled from her room. "I think it's time." Lucas ran to her side.

"I'll get Miss Sarah to stay with Gigi." Lucas called the main house, and Sarah Jane came running over.

"I'm here, Mr. Lucas. You can take Miss Lilly to the hospital to have that baby. We're all excited to see her. Don't worry; we have everything under control."

"Thanks, Miss Sarah." Lucas put his hand on Lilly's back and escorted her out to his car.

Lucas raced to the hospital and Lilly was taken back immediately. As the doctor examined Lilly, Lucas's heart pounded. His hands were sweaty, and his neck was damp. "You got this princess!" He stood to the side of her and held her hand.

"It's time," the doctor said. Lucas gasped for air. Panic filled his chest as Lilly squeezed his hand tight. Suddenly, the room went black.

"Great! Just great! He passes out on me!"

Moments later, a nurse tended to Lucas while Lilly pushed one final time. "What happened?" Lucas looked at the nurse.

"You okay, sir?"

"Yeah, I ..." Then he heard his daughter crying. "Is that—" He had a wave of emotion come over him. *I'm a father now. It's real. She's here. Oh, God, I am a father!* He collected himself and went to Lilly's side. "She's got my nose." Lucas touched his baby's head.

"She has a cute nose."

"We're parents now, Lils. We're no longer just the two of us."

"Three of a kind, just in time," Lilly said in a sing-song voice. Jesi looked at her mom and grasped her pinky. "My little hummingbird. I love her with all of my heart."

"I do, too," Lucas said and tenderly brushed Jesi's cheek with his pinky. "We have another Crusader amongst us." Lucas chuckled as Jesi yawned. "She's the best thing in the world. Just think, Lils, we made that."

"We sure did. We're forever connected, Lukie."

"That we are Lils; that we are." He chuckled. "We have to teach her how to be a Crusader."

"She's going to be the best Crusader." Lilly cooed.

Although Jesi had been in perfect health at the hospital, when she had been home for a few days she wouldn't stop crying. "Come on, hummingbird; it's okay. Mommy's here." Lilly rocked Jesi to sleep, but, as soon as she stopped, Jesi would start up again. "Something is wrong with her. I don't know what to do," she told Helen, who she hoped knew something that would help.

"Let me hold her." Helen reached out her arms. "I feel Jesse close when I hold her." Lilly handed the baby to her, and Helen felt something on the back of Jesi's head. "Come here. Feel this." Lilly cautiously put her hand on the back of Jesi's head at the base of her neck. "You feel that lump?"

"Yeah, what's causing that?" Lilly felt the back of her own neck. "I don't have it. I wonder if Lucas has it? Now I'm worried."

"She'll be fine. You have first-time, new-mom anxieties. You'll have that for the rest of your life," Helen chuckled. "Then you'll have more kids and grandkids and continue it with them. But you're strong and resilient. You have this, Lilly bug." Lilly smiled at the use of the nickname Jesse used to call her.

"I miss him too. He was such a good man. I can't wait to tell her all about him."

The next day when Lilly took Jesi for her examination the doctors noticed how dehydrated she was with her sunken eyes and dry mouth. Jesi was admitted. "We'll get some fluids in her, and she'll be better soon," the attending doctor explained. "That bump on the back of her neck?" Lilly asked the doctor.

"That I'm a little more concerned about. I'm going to have to take some x-rays and blood work and see what's going on."

"What do you think it could be?"

"I don't know yet."

While Jesi was in the hospital, Lucas tended to Helen. She had been strong, but Lucas could see she was getting weaker. Lucas was exhausted, and, as he sat by Helen's bedside, he couldn't help but think of his mother. *Mama.* He wiped stray tears from his face. *She's going to be with you soon. Help me deal with everything. I need you now.* A phantom scent of lavender filled the air as he felt a warm comforting breeze blow through the room. *I'll Always Love You* came on the radio. Lucas had a flashback of a woman singing it to him. He could hear the words "I love you, Luca," and the phantom scent grew stronger. "Thanks, Mama." Lucas smiled and sat back.

JUST THE TWO OF US

After a couple of days, Jesi recovered from the dehydration and was able to come home. Lucas picked Lilly up from the hospital. "What did the doctors say?"

"They don't have an answer yet." Lilly sighed. "How's Gigi?" Lilly got in the car.

"She's getting weaker. She's having problems breathing. So, being around this angel is just what I need." He snuggled Jesi then put her in her car seat.

"You spend as much time with Gigi as possible. You make those memories. She doesn't need to be alone. I'll take care of Jesi."

"Thank you, Lilly; I appreciate it."

"I wonder if anyone's told John?"

"I don't know. He hasn't spoken to me. I don't know if he'll want to speak to me, but I know she wants him to do her funeral." Lucas said.

"Does he know that?"

"I don't know. I think it's time for people to start making their way to see her."

"I'll call Sheryl when we get home," Lilly said.

The next day, Lilly and Lucas got a call to come to the doctor's office. The doctor was concerned. *Everything is going to be okay,* Lilly consoled herself. *I have faith. Mama G told me to hold onto my faith. Uncle John preaches on faith. Please, God, let my baby be okay.*

"She's going to be fine, Lils. She's a Crusader. Crusaders are tough. Remember that."

"She's got to be okay, Lukie."

Lilly and Lucas were sitting in the doctor's office when another doctor came in. "This is Dr. Dixon. He's an oncologist I referred Jessica to." Jesi's pediatrician introduced. "Hello, Miss Patrick, Mr. Ashton." He nodded to them and sat down.

"We've run several MRIs, CAT scans, and blood work. We don't have a good prognosis."

"What do you mean, doctor?" Lucas asked and squeezed Lilly's hand.

"Jessica has a rare brain tumor."

"Oh, no!" Lilly gasped and raised her hand to her mouth. "But you can do surgery, right?"

"I'm sorry, Miss Patrick; it's inoperable."

"What?!" Lucas stood up, his fists by his side. "That's not possible!"

"It's a rare glioma cancer that I've never seen in a child this young."

"What—" Lilly didn't know what she wanted to ask. She held her breath, waiting for the doctor to say more.

Dr. Dixon looked at her; his face clearly showing empathy. "I'm so sorry. She only has weeks to live."

"NO! She can't die on us! Not now! Not my Jesi!" Lilly cried.

"I'm so sorry. There's no cure for this type of cancer. Please try to enjoy the time you have left with her."

"But she's a baby! There's got to be something you can do. Something someone can do. I'll donate blood tissues—anything to save her!" Lilly pleaded.

"I'm sorry, Miss Patrick. There's nothing we can do."

"Thank you, doctor. Can we see her?" Lucas asked.

"Yes, she's in NICU."

Lilly and Lucas walked in a daze back to the NICU. Jesi was hooked up to tubes and monitors, sleeping.

"What else, Lukie?! What else can go wrong?"

"I don't know, Lilly. I don't know."

Lucas tried to be strong. He paced in a daze and pulled on his hair and wiped away the tears he couldn't hold back. At the same time he wanted to hold Lilly and spend every moment with Jesi before she, too, was gone, and he needed to be by Gigi's side. *Who do I spend my time with? They're both dying. My family is leaving me. Mama, what did I ever do to lose everyone?* Lucas and Lilly needed the support of a family, but they were cut off as if they were rabid animals. Once again, all they had was each other. Just the two of them.

Lilly seemed to sense his struggle. "I'll stay with her," she said. "You stay with Helen. Helen has no one. Jesi has me."

"What about you?"

"I'll be okay." Lilly wiped the tears from her face. "I'm going to change. I'm going to be tough and strong. If I had been strong, none of this would have happened. You would still be with Mary, and John, and Sheryl wouldn't hate us. If I hadn't given in to my fear, then none of this would be happening, and this little angel wouldn't pay for my mistake. No, I'm done. I'm going to be tough. I'm going to be a fighter. You can't be in both places, and it's my fault you have to choose, so I'm taking the choice away from you."

"Liliana."

"No, I mean it, Lucas. Spend your time with Helen. She's your grandmother."

"Yes, and Jesi is my DAUGHTER. She's mine, too, Liliana."

"I know. I just ... I don't want to make you have to pick."

"I can spend my days with Gigi, and then I can come here and spend the night."

"I worry about you. I can handle it. It's all my fault anyway," Lilly admitted.

"It's not your fault. You didn't force me."

"You were only doing it to be a great friend."

"I'd do it again, too. I'd do anything for you, Liliana. I hope you know that."

"And I would for you, too." They held each other tightly.

It had been a couple of weeks since the diagnosis. Life was hard, but they'd developed a routine. Lucas spent his days with Helen, the evenings he spent with Jesi forcing Lilly to go home and get some sleep. Lilly tried to be strong, but she became morose. Her depression was understandably in full force. Lucas had to be strong for everyone.

"How can it keep going?" Lilly asked, melancholy.

"What do you mean?" Lucas asked.

"How can the world keep turning when everything is dying around us?"

"Because it has to go on. Do you want something to eat?" he asked her.

"No, I can't eat."

"Lils, you haven't eaten all day."

"I'm not hungry," she admitted.

"You have to eat; otherwise, you're going to wind up in the hospital, too."

"No one would care if I wound up in the hospital," she mumbled.

"I would care," Lucas told her.

"You shouldn't. I'm not worth caring about."

"I made a promise to you as a little boy, and I'm keeping it. Crusaders pledge, Lilly." He reached out his hand, but Lilly just stared out the window, lost in despair. "Crusaders pledge, LILIANA!"

"What does it matter? A little pledge we made as kids. What good has it done?"

"It's kept me hopeful and alive many times," Lucas admitted.

"Has it?"

"It has, because I knew there was a girl that would fight to the end to keep me safe. Now come on, Liliana, Crusaders pledge!"

Lucas's anger spurred her to give a half-hearted answer. "I promise to protect you with all my heart at all times," she said.

"You think you're the only one hurting?! I'M LOSING EVERYONE!!!" Lucas bellowed in the hospital room. "I have no one, Liliana!!! No one! You have John. You have Sheryl. You even have Matthew. Even if they're all crap, they're still there! I have no one. No. One. Not one. Single. Person. Left!! So, I'm sorry. I can't let you wallow in this! You haven't slept in days. You haven't bathed in three days. You stare out the window while your daughter needs her mother! She is fighting with what little life she has, and you're sitting here wallowing."

Lilly looked at him broken hearted, and they fell apart.

"It's okay, princess; I got you." Lucas held onto her as she wrapped her arms around him, crying. "Lukie."

"I know," he whispered in her ear, his hand on the back of her head.

"Everyone—" she sobbed.

"I know," he choked back.

"Just us..."

"I know, honey. I know. It's just the two of us. It will always be just the two of us. We'll always be together. Remember, Crusaders forever?"

"Crusaders forever," she repeated.

"Now, let's get you cleaned up and get something to eat."

As the end of July rolled around, Lilly fluctuated between bouts of depression and anger. One day, she found a Bible in the hospital room, probably left by a hospital volunteer, and it triggered the worst of her emotions. She couldn't bear staying in the room for another second. Blindly, she stomped down the hall, not paying attention to where she was going, yet found herself outside the hospital's chapel. Her hands curled into fists, her anger at a tipping point, she studied the polished pews, the picture-perfect altar, the picture of Jesus she used to be so fond of. The longer she stood there, the angrier she got. "I don't believe in you anymore!" she yelled and stomped towards the altar. "I don't believe! You could have helped me. I begged you when I was six years old and scared to death because my daddy hurt me. I begged you to make it stop, but there was nothing. Now Lucas is losing everything. He's losing all his family, and he's barely eighteen years old. He's alone. He has no family at all. Why would you do this?" She took a seat in a pew and glared up at the cross.

"Maybe because he knows the future better than you do." Lilly turned around to find a woman standing there. She had white hair and was wearing a white trench coat, white clothing, and a gold tie. "Maybe he's doing it so you'll make the choices he needs you to make."

"Choices? Choices? What choices? I have no choice. My daughter is dying! He could stop it, but He won't."

"Your daughter's death can save someone else's life."

"Why can't she live?" Lilly questioned pleadingly.

"Is it better to let seven people live, and one person die or let one person live, and seven people die?" she asked.

"Well, duh. It's better to let seven people live." Lilly rolled her eyes.

"Even if the one person who is dying is a baby?"

"That's not fair! She's innocent! She hasn't done anything!"

"By her death, she might save someone else, someone you love more than anything."

"There's no one I love more than my daughter!"

"What if her death is a catalyst for a cure for the cancer that ails her?"

"How did you know she has cancer?"

"What if, by her death, you change your mind and decide to become a doctor after all? What if one of the buildings you want to design crumbles and kills a lot of people."

Lilly gasped. Only Lucas knew she was going to follow her dream of being an architect after all.

"Who are you?"

"What if, by her death, you save another family from the pain you're going through?"

"Who ... how ...?"

"Think about that, my darling Liliana. It's a pivotal time for you right now. Don't throw away all that you believe in. Don't give into the anger, the rage. Give into the peace. Accept the peace. You don't know what the future holds. Give into the one that does. Give into the Future Maker." She turned around to walk away.

"Wait," Lilly turned and called after her.

The woman turned around and said, "It's your decision," and walked away before Lilly could say anything more.

Lilly stood there with her mouth open with so many questions running through her mind. *What if Jesi's death was a catalyst for change and help? What if Jesi's cancer could be cured in the future? What if someone else is going through the same thing, but I can help them?*

Lilly collapsed back down in the pew and bowed her head. Fear replaced the rage and anger she felt. "Did I go too far?" Lilly trembled. "I'm so scared. I don't hate you. I just ... why my daughter? Why? Why?" Lilly looked around for the mysterious woman, but there was no one there. She felt herself trembling.

Always believe, baby. Elizabeth's words rang in her head as she turned back to face the cross. *You have to believe and have faith, baby. No matter what happens, God has a reason for it. You have to have faith.*

"Oh, Mama G," Lilly whispered. "I could use your faith now." Lilly bowed her head and said a prayer for everyone. A warm peace came over her, and she wiped her tears away. She suddenly felt acceptance for everything in her life, the good times and the bad. Lilly was barely seventeen years old, but it felt like her whole future just fell into place.

Chapter Twenty-One

It was now August. They had brought Jesi home, and hospice had been called in for both Jesi and Helen. John, Sheryl, and Matthew visited both of them several times. John sang and prayed for them. Sheryl helped Helen with her burial outfit. It was an awkward time. Sheryl was kind, but John was stoic. Most of the time, Lucas and Lilly stayed away to let them spend time with the two of them

Lucas called Elizabeth to give an update on Helen. He needed to hear her voice. He needed to talk to Jacob. He didn't say anything about being a father. He didn't want them to be disappointed, but Elizabeth comforted him just like she did when he was a little boy. She gave him strength. But Lucas could feel his rage building. He struck his pillow, but it wasn't enough. He threw it on the floor and stomped on it. "Why?! Why?! Why?!" He thundered and then cleared the bookshelf with a sweep of his arms, before falling to his knees, racked with mental pain.

"I just feel like everything is my fault, and I'm being punished."

"A lot of things have happened, and it will take some time to heal. But, trust me, your Uncle John loves you like nothing else," Sheryl comforted her.

"Does he?"

"Yes, baby, he does. You're his squirrel," Sheryl reminded her.

"I don't think I'm *squirrel* anymore." Lilly looked down sadly.

"You'll always be my squirrel, Liliana." John came over to her. "I'm sorry I've treated you so badly."

"It's okay; I deserved it. I hurt Mary. I know what I'd do if someone hurt my Jesi, but I do love you."

John wrapped his arms around her; Lilly sobbed into his shoulder.

"It's just some things happened we can't talk about, so it's best to just distance ourselves from each other. I am sorry you're going through all of this, though."

"Please don't be mad at Lucas. He was only being a friend to me."

"It's a tough situation all around." John held onto Lilly. "Don't think I ever stopped loving you. I'll always love you. Don't give up on your faith. Hold on to that with everything, even though it's going to be tested tremendously. Be strong, Liliana, because it's going to be a long, bumpy road here the next few months."

"I will." Lilly wiped her eyes and hugged him.

Everyone sat around Helen as she lay there with her eyes closed. The nurse checked her vitals. "It's only a matter of moments now. She can still hear you, if you want to say something."

Lucas rubbed Helen's hand gently. "I love you, Gigi. I love you with all my heart. Say hi to Mama for me." He choked back tears as Lilly took his other hand.

"I have you, Lukie. Crusaders pledge," she whispered. Lucas entwined their fingers together and squeezed her hand.

"Let's say a prayer that she has a peaceful passing," John announced to everyone. He took Helen's hand and closed his eyes. "Father, please welcome our beloved Helen into heaven, where she joins her husband Jesse and her daughter Celeste. Please give her grandson Lucas comfort and all those who loved her." He was silent momentarily, then sang a hymn that was one of Helen's favorites.

"Thank you, John. I think she'd appreciate that," Lucas said.

"I am so sorry for all that you are going through. I do wish you the best."

"Thank you," Lucas said softly.

The cuckoo clock sounded midnight. Lilly squeezed Lucas's hand as the heart monitor flat-lined.

Lucas dropped his head and squeezed Helen's hand. "Goodbye, Gigi," he said softly and kissed her forehead. Everyone gathered around Lucas and held him up.

"She was like a mom to us," Matthew told him. Everyone sat quietly as the nurse tended to Helen. A few moments later, the funeral attendant came and took Helen away.

"They're going to have to do that to my baby soon," Lilly cried.

John wrapped his arm around her. "It's so not fair. Do you think she knows how loved she is?"

"I think she does. Just spend as much time with her as you can."

"She's my sole focus." Lilly laid her head on John's shoulder. "I feel so sorry for Lucas. He's losing everyone."

"He has you," John reminded her.

"He'll always have me. I'll never leave him."

"I wish I had a friend like you. You're a true friend, Liliana. Don't ever get jaded and let that go."

"Uncle John, would God let something happen to Jesi so that it would change my future?"

Chapter Twenty-Two

Lucas looked at Helen in the casket. She had chosen a dark green casket with light green upholstery, and she wore green satin pajamas and a dark, grey-speckled wig. Her hands were crossed over her abdomen. She looked young for her age. A green floral spray with little white flowers, predominantly daisies and roses, covered the lower portion of the casket.

"I hope I was a good grandson to you, Gigi. I hope I made you proud. Now, you're with my mom and Grandpa, and you'll be with my daughter soon. When she gets there, please tell her she is loved. Tell her I love her more than anything. Welcome her with open arms, as I'm sure Mom is opening her arms to you. Please guide me and my future. Please be with me for the rest of my life. Please never abandon me. I will always love you." Lucas momentarily put his hand on hers and then looked at all the flowers sent from friends and loved ones. While they couldn't come, Elizabeth and Jacob sent a dozen purple tulips with their condolences.

Lucas sat in quiet contemplation for a few moments. *I'm alone now. It's just me.* He wrung his hands at the realization. *Remember, son, always be strong.* Matthew's lesson rang in his ears. Lucas stood up, pulled his jacket down, buttoned it, checked his tie, and made sure the ribbon on his lapel was straight. He cleared his throat and put on his business persona. He had faced a lot in his young eighteen years, but he would always be strong. There was no taking him down. "I can do this! I can face this!" He opened the door and welcomed everyone in to pay their final respects to one Mrs. Helen Justine Cast Thompson.

After the ceremony was over and the condolences were accepted, Lilly took Lucas's hand, and they went home. Lucas checked on Jesi, then went straight to his bedroom and cried his heart out.

Now, I'll never know anything about my mom. And I have to go tomorrow to plan my daughter's funeral. God, why are you doing this to me? What did I ever do that was so bad to make me go through this? I'm eighteen, and I have no family. Why do you hate me?

Lucas opened the Bible Elizabeth gave him as a child. *Blessed are they who mourn, for they will be comforted.* This verse always gave him comfort when he missed his mom. He turned to Psalms and read verse 62:8. This was the first verse Elizabeth taught him. *Always trust in God, Lulu. Pour out your heart to him. He is our refuge.* The day had been exhaustingly long, but it was over. *Ease my troubled mind, please.* Lucas continued to read. Before he knew it, he was lulled into a peaceful sleep.

Lilly watched Jesi sleep. *I want to remember as much about you as I can.* She squeezed the little bird she sewed. It played Lucas's song and her hummingbird song. Jesi reached for it. "Yeah, that's your daddy singing to you. You're his baby bluebird. He loves you, baby. You're mommy's hummingbird, and I love you." Jesi looked at Lilly. "Yes, my hummingbird. How's mommy's hummingbird?" Jesi kicked her legs

Lilly sang her hummingbird song and then said to no one in particular, "I need to get some hummingbird feeders. I need two. One for each month she was alive. I want to put a hummingbird and a blue bird on her headstone. She'll always be my hummingbird. I might get a hummingbird tattoo on my heart. Tea, I didn't make Lukie's tea."

"I don't need tea," he said.

"Doesn't matter; I need to make it." Lilly refilled everyone's coffee cup and made Lucas his tea. Then she sat down and took a bite of her pancakes. "I don't have enough syrup. Does anyone need anything?" She looked around the table.

"Liliana, you don't have to do anything," Matthew told her.

"I know, but ... I have to make her proud. I want her to look down on me and be proud that I'm her mom. I don't want her to see me wallowing around. She needs to see me be strong and taking care of those that I love."

"Squirrel, we're fine," John told her.

"Here, Uncle John, let me get you a tomato. I know you like tomatoes with your eggs—oh, grits—I don't have grits. I'm sorry. I would have made them." Lilly sliced the tomato into easier-to-eat pieces and put it on John's plate. "Let's see ... what else?" Lilly sat down for a minute, then got up and started doing dishes.

"Honey, I can get those for you," Sheryl told her.

"No, it's okay. You're a guest in my house." Lilly smiled at Sheryl.

Suddenly a loud crash of thunder broke the mood. When the rain started, Lilly looked at John and fell to the floor in tears.

"Is it leaking in here?" Lucas wiped his neck and looked up at the ceiling. "The back of my neck is soaked, but I don't see anything."

Sheryl's voice got shaky. "That's your tears. Jesi couldn't go to heaven with your tears on her face, so they came back to your neck."

"How do you know?" Lucas asked.

"It happened with me and my mom. I wiped my tears on her forehead, and after she passed, my neck got wet. She's in heaven now." Sheryl wiped her eyes and hugged Lucas.

"My baby, Aunt Sheryl, my baby. My daughter is gone," Lucas cried. Sheryl held him.

"I'm alone," Lucas said softly. "I have no family left." Sheryl looked at John, who shook his head no.

"You're not alone, Lucas. You have me, you have John, and you have Lilly. You have us all."

"Crusaders promise, Lukie. I mean it, Lucas. I will always remain faithful to you. Crusaders forever." Lilly wrapped her arms around him. "I love you," Lilly said.

"I love you too," Lucas answered.

It had been a long night with no sleep. Lilly sat on the terrace holding one of Jesi's teddy bears. Lucas sat beside her with the plush blue bird he had got for Jesi. They sat on the patio and watched the hazy sunrise. "She would be two months old today. She had so much to look forward to. Her first word, her first tooth, walking, crawling. We'll never have that. I don't think I'll ever have kids again. Is it fair to have kids after this? I'll have to go to the library and see if there's a word that describes parents that lose a child," Lilly said.

"It's called painful and indescribable," Lucas said.

"Unbearable."

"Miserable."

"Horrible," Lilly added. "Terrible," she continued.

"I've run out of *ibble* words." Lucas laughed.

"Undesirable," Lilly added.

"There you go," he chuckled. "Is it okay to laugh? Will it ever be okay to laugh?"

"I think she'd want us to. She'd want us to smile and laugh. She'd want us to be happy. I want to decorate her grave with all kinds of childhood things she'll never get to experience. I want balloons and animals and little dolls. I want to take her bird I made her and put it in her casket."

"I want to keep the little blue bird I got her. I want something to hold that she held," Lucas said.

"Oh, my sweet Jesi," Lilly choked. Lucas squeezed her hand. Lilly sat upright and set her jaw. "I'm going to do it." She wiped her face.

"Do what?"

"I'm going to find a cure. I'm going to do it. I will go to my grave with my name in the medical journals next to the cure for cancer. I'm not letting anyone else go through this. No other mother is going to feel the pain I feel right now. I refuse to let it happen."

"I thought you were going to be an architect and design my office building?"

"What if the building I design crumbles and people get killed? No, I'm going to do it. I'm going to find the cure for cancer. Crusaders promise," Lilly said confidently.

"But your dream is to be an architect," Lucas reminded her.

"Screw my dreams."

"Liliana!"

"No. I'm not letting her death be in vain. I'm going to do it. I'm going to find a cure if it's the last thing I do."

"When are you going to start?"

"I don't know," Lilly sighed. "It's too late to start school for this year."

"Are you even in the mindset?"

"No. You?"

"No, but I have to do something. I promised Gigi I would go to school."

"I vow to Jesi I'm going to be the best doctor I can be. Crusader goals."

"Crusader goals?" he asked.

"I want to do something in Jesi's honor."

"Me, too," Lucas added.

"What can we do?"

"Start a scholarship in her honor," Lucas said.

"I'm going to save a child in her honor. I'm going to work my ass off and save someone in her honor. We should make a list." Lilly walked back into the kitchen, and Lucas followed her. "Aha. Found it," she said, taking out a notepad and sitting at the table. "Crusaders Goals Pledge. Goal one: cure cancer."

"You really think you're going to do that?"

"I will do everything in my power to do it."

"Shouldn't you set a more realistic goal?" Lucas asked.

"Save someone with cancer. Is that better?"

"Sounds more realistic," he chuckled. "Although if there's anyone who can cure cancer, it would be you."

"Goal two."

"Shouldn't we put graduate college as the first goal?" He chuckled.

"Goal three: graduate college, then."

"What's goal two?"

"Go to college." She laughed. "Goal four?"

"Set up the Jessica Lauren Patrick Ashton Memorial Scholarship."

"What do they need to study?"

"Science, Architecture, or business management."

"Goal five?"

"Laugh without feeling guilty."

"Goal six?"

"Do something special in her honor."

"What can we do?"

"Donate to a bird sanctuary."

"I like that since she's our little bird. Goal seven?"

"Help people that have an addiction. In my mom's honor."

"Goal eight?"

"How many are we going to set?" Lucas asked.

"Ten sound good? Nice even number?"

"Um, I can't think of any more."

"Change someone's world for the better, even if it's just a little act of kindness," Lilly added.

"Goal nine?"

"Set up a scholarship in my mom's honor."

"Okay, goal ten. Always try to be together on her birthday," Lilly wrote.

"We're together all the time, anyway."

"I know, but we make a special effort on that day. Since school and other things can interfere." She made a copy of the list and dated it.

"Here's your copy, and here's mine. I say we get together every year on Jesi's birthday and see how far we've come in our goals."

"I agree," Lucas said.

"Crusaders shake." They did their special handshake, then Lilly put her list in her favorite book and Lucas put his in his wallet. "I need to go to the store. Will you go with me? I want to pick out some fabric and make her a special blanket to be buried in."

"Can we get some green and blue fabric?"

"I think we can do that. We can see if we can find a print with baby birds."

"I like that. Lils …?"

"Yeah?"

"Are we going to be okay?"

"What do you mean?"

"Are we going to get through this together?"

"We have no choice. We're Crusaders. We can face anything. Look what we have faced."

"I know. Crusaders pledge?" Lucas asked.

"I promise to protect you with all my heart at all times."

At that moment, sadness hit them like a wave. They held each other tight, filled with solidarity over grief for their precious daughter. Their little bird.

"We'll be okay. We're tough cookies. We're Crusaders, and Crusaders always bounce back."

"Yes, we do, Lukie. Yes, we do."

While Lilly made a wish and blew out her candles, Lucas looked around at the lake house. "This isn't home anymore," he admitted.

"Has it ever been home?"

"Not really. My home is in New York. I'll always think of New York as home."

"Are you going to go back there?" Lilly asked, afraid of the answer.

"I want to," he admitted.

"I don't blame you."

"Why don't you go with me?" he asked hopeful.

"Because this is my home. This is where she is at."

"What are we going to do?" Lucas asked timidly.

"Follow our dreams," Lilly stated.

"You can always go back with me. You can go to school there," he coaxed.

"I know I should, but ..." she looked around, "you've been held back by me all your life. Maybe ... maybe it's time you fly, my little bird." She looked at him in tears.

"I don't want to leave you." His eyes welled up.

"I'll be okay. She's here, Lukie. I'm not ready to leave her. But we have to keep in touch," she demanded.

"We will. Crusaders promise?"

"Crusaders promise." They held hands and lovingly did their special handshake.

As Lucas turned nineteen, he was accepted at a college in New York. He was going to start in the spring quarter in March. He'd once again be near Elizabeth and Jacob. As they have done every day, Lucas and Lilly made the trip to see their daughter. This time bringing pink flowers and balloons to her grave.

"I love you, my hummingbird," Lilly said, a gentle breeze blowing through her hair. "I like to think breezes are God's whisper of love."

"That's a nice thought." Lucas took her hand and squeezed it as a breeze blew through his hair, too. A tear streamed down his face. "Shall we go?"

"Yeah, I have to make your dinner. I bought a special pasta maker just for today."

"Thank you for making it for me." Lucas smiled at her.

"I'll always make it for you." She smiled, took his hand, and walked away from their daughter's grave.

As they drove down the gravel road towards home, Lucas mused, "Look how far we've come."

"We've overcome a lot."

"And we've done it together," Lucas reminded her.

"We'll always be together," Lilly said confidently.

"Where there's one ..." Lucas started their famous phrase.

"There's the other," they said in unison.

"Just the two of us," Lucas said.

"Just the two of us."

Epilogue

Lucas packed the last of his things and closed the trunk. Lilly tried not to cry. "This is it, princess." He smiled bravely at her.

"You be careful! Call me when you get there and get settled," she demanded.

"I will. You call me if you need anything."

"Promise you'll keep in touch."

"I promise," Lucas said.

"Good luck in school."

"Promise me you'll enroll." He looked at her.

"I promise."

"Promise me you'll be okay and not get too down." Lucas wanted assurance.

"I will. Promise me you'll come back and see me some time."

"I will." He smiled.

"Crusaders promise?"

"Crusaders promise."

"I love you, Lucas. Thanks for everything all these years."

"I love you, too, Liliana. Thanks for always being my friend." Lucas pulled her close to him, and they cried hard. "Well," he sighed, "I better go. Are you sure you don't want to go with me?" He had to ask one final time.

"I'm not ready to leave her yet."

"Don't think bad about me leaving." He needed reassurance.

"I could never think anything bad about you." Lucas leaned over and kissed her cheek.

"Goodbye, Liliana, my princess."

"Goodbye, Lucas, my Lukie." Lilly cried her eyes out. Lucas got in the car and waved until she was out of view.

Lucas arrived in New York a few hours later. He took a deep breath and felt a calm come over him as he drove down the street. Some things had changed, but some remained the same. He walked up to the porch and knocked on the door of a house he hadn't seen since he was eleven years old. He was nervous about how they would react.

Here it goes, Ashton. What are you going to walk into? Will they welcome me? What if they turn me away? Will I have a family again? Should I have done this? Should I have called first? God, Ashton, this is it, man!

After what seemed like forever, the door opened, and Elizabeth stood there.

"Oh, my gosh! Lucas!!" She looked at him, shocked. Elizabeth opened her arms. "Come here, Lulu!" She hugged him to within an inch of his life.

"Oh, Mama G." He held onto her tightly. Life was good again. He was home.

Crusaders Forever

Two best friends, forever and a day
Our love and friendship will never stray
Through thick and thin, we'll always be
Two best friends for eternity.
Lucas Ashton, age 11
Liliana Patrick, age 10
Crusaders Forever!
I promise to protect you with all my heart at all times Crusaders Pledge.

A Note From The Author

Thank you so much for reading! I hope you enjoyed part one of our journey through Lilly and Lucas's life. Follow along on the next phase of their life, young adulthood. How will Lilly and Lucas cope with being separated? How will college life be with Lucas and the Glasses? What have Elizabeth and Jacob been up to? Will dreams come true? Will an old flame reignite? Follow along with Lucas and Lilly in book two *The Bitter Journey* coming soon!

Thank you to the following people. You mean the world to me!

Charlie Osborne for being my sounding board and supporter. I love you, little brother.

For Princess Kaylee Susan, sissy's Littlest Girl, who I miss dearly. You always sat on my chest while I wrote and gave me comfort and inspiration. I'll see you at Rainbow Bridge someday.

For Norman Bates and Meeko Starr. I love both of you so much! You've given me so much joy. Norman always sitting on my laptop making sure I don't get writer's block and Meeko sitting at my feet. You are the best cat and dog team ever! I love both of sissy's babies.

To Ronnie for formatting and being a great friend during all of this. For helping me with the steps to publish this. Look it's done!

To Amy Smith and Chrystal Martin. Thank you for reading my little excerpts and giving advice. You guys are the best.

To Trina Blankenship for reading the original version. Look how far I've come! Thank you for reading it in all it's crazy glory.

To my online friends. Thank you for the encouragement and belief in me. When I felt down you kept me sane.

And lastly to my Alpaca Hoes. You ladies are awesome! I love you so much. You've been there for me through some of the hardest times. Thanks for seeing this through with me.

And mostly thank you God for giving me the ability to do this and for watching over me. For helping me when I feel down and for keeping my spirits up. For my salvation and for always, no matter what supplying my needs according to your riches in glory. I love you!

Philippians 4.19 for life!

And to you for reading and making my dream a reality. May you have the most blessed day ever!

Lisa

About The Author

I was the only Christmas present my parents could never return. That was always the joke. I was born in Alpena, MI. My family moved back to Wyandotte, MI when I was a little girl. A couple of years later my brother came along. When I was going on seven we made the big move to Kentucky. I grew up here but have my fondest memories of summers in Michigan, with my grandma, aunts, uncles, and cousins. I've always been a big sports fan. My Uncle Pete (RIP) used to laugh because he saw me as a little toddler reading the sports page. I will always follow my Michigan teams but my biggest passion is Big Blue. That was the passion I shared with my dad for the nineteen years I had him. There's not a March Madness that goes by that I don't think of him. I started writing at an early age. I wrote short stories and novellas never thinking anyone would want to read them. Then one day my mom had a heart attack. I was off work for a couple of months taking care of her. I returned to work and it was the middle of the night. It was time for my lunch break. I bought a notebook and pen and sat out in my car under the parking lot lights and started the first draft. It was

Milton Keynes UK
Ingram Content Group UK Ltd.
UKHW030951261124
451585UK00001B/41